D0249274

Stranger at the Window

Stranger at the Window

Vivien Alcock

Houghton Mifflin Company
Boston

C.2

First published as The Face at the Window in Great Britain by
Methuen Children's Books, an imprint of Reed Consumer Books Ltd.

Library of Congress Cataloging-in-Publication Data
Alcock, Vivien
[Face at the window]
The stranger at the window/by Vivien Alcock.—1st American ed.
p.   cm.
Summary: At first eleven-year-old Lesley doesn't like the three older
Harwood children who live next door to her aunt in London, but she
comes to see them differently when she is drawn into their efforts to
help a young boy who has entered the country illegally.
RNF ISBN 0-395-81661-0   PAP ISBN 0-395-94329-9
[1. Illegal aliens—Fiction. 2. Friendship—Fiction. 3. Family life—London
(England)—Fiction. 4. London (England)—Fiction.]   I. Title
A334SvPZ7.   1998
[Fic]—dc21   97-14195   CIP   AC

Printed in the United States of America
HAD   10 9 8 7 6 5 4 3 2 1

To Miriam Hodgson, the best of editors,
with thanks for all her help and encouragement

1

It was there again, watching me. I could not tell whether it was a girl or a boy. It was just a face, dark-eyed, sallow-skinned, with black hair that merged into the shadows behind it. When it saw me looking at it, it vanished behind the curtain of the attic window in the house next door.

Before it moved, I'd thought it was a mask, put there by one of the young Harwoods to get me back for having watched them. Victoria, probably; it seemed her style. Christopher and Robert, I thought, were too old to have bothered with such childish tit for tat.

I often used to sit by my bedroom window when I first came to live with my aunt. From here, I could see into the garden next door and even, if I leaned forward and pressed my forehead against the glass, into the room where they sat, reading and watching television. I don't know why they fascinated me so. I was lonely, I suppose.

It's so dull and quiet here, I'd written to my mother.

It was true. I knew nobody in London except Auntie Amy, and she'd always seemed a strange person to me. She was much older than my mother; you wouldn't think they were sisters. Before I came, she'd lived alone in this big old house, with empty rooms all around her. She never said things like "Finish up your food, dear," or "Wrap up warm," or "Isn't it time you were in bed?" I sometimes wondered if she remembered that I'd been ill and should be looked after carefully, although I knew my mother had told her this before she left.

"I daren't take Lesley with me," my mother had said. "Cairo's the most unhealthy city in the world. She'd be bound to catch anything going. She's been so ill, poor child. I hate to leave her, but I can't afford to turn down this job. And I know you'll take care of her for me, won't you, Amy dear?"

"Of course I will," my aunt had promised, but she must have forgotten. She treated me as if I were as old as she was, and as sensible, which I am not.

If I'd been sensible, I'd have known that Christopher, Robert, and Victoria Harwood wouldn't want to be friends with me. I was not their type. They were everything I'd always wanted to be, good-looking and self-assured. They spoke in clear, loud voices, as if they didn't care who heard them.

They didn't like being watched, however. One day, glancing up, Victoria saw me at my window. She scowled and muttered something to the others. Before they turned round to look up at me, I dodged behind my curtain out of sight — just like the face that watched me now.

Who could it be? Not one of them. I'd seen it at the attic window when they were all in the garden. Not their cleaner. She was old and cheerful, while the face was young and sad. The face of a prisoner. Could they keep somebody locked up in their attic? You don't expect the people living next door to do such things, but I wouldn't have put anything past Victoria.

She looks nice enough. Her cheeks and eyes shine as if they've been polished. Her brown hair is crisp and curling, and her teeth very white. She looks like a red Delicious apple, but she's never been sweet to me. I think she has a maggot in her heart.

One morning, after I'd been in London only a few days, Auntie Amy said, in her soft, vague voice,

"I'm afraid I'm very quiet, Lesley. It must be dull for you. But there're some nice children next door, two older boys and a girl about your age. Would you like to invite them over to tea? I thought you'd like to have some young company."

I wanted to say, "No! Not yet. I'm not ready." This was before I'd seen the face. I still admired the bright young Harwoods then, whom I'd seen, laughing and shouting to each other in their garden. Next to them, I knew I would appear colorless, as thin and pale and lank as a noodle. "Wait till the weather's warmer," I wanted to say. "Wait till I'm fatter and have some color in my cheeks. Wait till I'm ready."

But I didn't say this. I just said, "How can I? I've never met them. They won't know who I am."

"I'll do it for you, shall I?" she asked.

I hesitated, then I said, "All right. Thanks."

So she asked them. It wasn't a success. She'd invited their mother too, and their mother did most of the talking. Mrs. Harwood ("Call me Kate," she'd said, but I didn't call her anything) was a tall, thin woman, with the same loud voice her children had. Her cheeks were red, like her daughter's, but rougher. Her eyes were blue, not brown. She waved her hands about when she talked. Once she knocked the spoon out of the sugar bowl, scattering sugar all over the table. "Clumsy me," she said, laughing and brushing the spilled sugar onto the carpet. My mother, though she's untidy, would have shouted if I'd done that, but Auntie Amy only smiled.

While the grown-ups were talking together, Christopher turned to me. He had a fairish stubble on his chin and upper lip as if he were growing a beard. I wondered how old he was. He looked completely grown-up to me. He asked politely how long I was going to be here.

"I don't know," I said. "It depends how long my mother's job in Cairo lasts."

"What does she do?"

"She works for V.A.G. Engineering."

"Oh," he said, losing interest, and glanced at his brother, as if to say, "Your turn now."

"What school do you go to?" Robert asked. He was not as good-looking as his brother. His brown hair was bushy, and his thick eyebrows nearly met over his nose, giving him a scowling look.

"I'm starting at Redwood next term," I told him.

"Redwood — that's the local comprehensive, isn't it?" he asked.

"Yes."

"I believe it's supposed to be quite good," he said politely.

I bet he didn't go to Redwood. I bet he went somewhere expensive.

I looked at Victoria and found her staring at me. She didn't smile. If it was her turn to ask a question, she ignored it and said nothing, so I decided to ask one of my own.

"How old are you?" I said.

You'd think I'd insulted her, the way she looked at me. I thought she wasn't going to answer, but then she said coldly, "I'm fourteen, if it really concerns you," and turned away to talk to Robert about some film she'd seen and I hadn't.

So she was about three years older than I. What of it? It's not a crime to be young, is it? Auntie Amy must be ages older than I, but she had said, "I'm sure we're going to be friends, Lesley."

They didn't stay long. They had other, more important things to do. Rehearsals for charity concerts to attend, rummage sales to collect for, rain forests to save. It was a wonder they managed to come at all, their lives were so busy and full of good works.

"You must come and see us soon, Lesley," their mother said before they left. "Just drop in any time. Don't wait for an invitation. After all, we only live next door. There's usually someone in, and the children will always be pleased to see you. Victoria's often wished there was another girl of her age nearby."

(You should have seen Victoria's face: she looked as disgusted as a cannibal being offered cauliflower with cheese.) *There's a girl and two older boys next door,* I wrote to my mother that night. *They came to tea today with their mum. She's as tall as a giraffe and has a voice like a trumpet. She asked me to call her Kate but I'm not going to. She asked me to come round to see them at any time, but I'm not going to do that either. They're all horrible. Stuck-up. Revolting. I'll never go knocking on their door. They'd have to beg me first. I can do without friends. I guess I'll have to. There's nobody else on the road at all. Not under ninety. I hate it here. Please send for me.*

I knew she wouldn't. I just wanted to make her feel bad for going off to Cairo and leaving me behind. She knows she is all I have.

Our house was very quiet and very empty, with only two of us in it. Auntie Amy worked at home. She made expensive lingerie for posh shops in Kensington, and she sat all day surrounded by fine silks and satins. The only time I saw her look dismayed was when I came into her workroom. She made me feel as if my hands were covered with grease and my feet in hobnailed boots.

"What is it, dear? Is there anything you want?" she'd ask nervously, drawing her silks away from me.

"I wondered if I could help you?"

"No, thank you, my dear."

So I'd go away, to wander through the empty rooms. In spite of what I told my mother, I did not really mind being lonely. When the weather was warm, I'd go out for a walk. Sometimes I'd meet the young Harwoods. Often they'd be carrying large cardboard boxes or plastic bags full of jumble or bundles of leaflets in their arms.

Victoria would grunt, "Hello," and walk quickly past me. Christopher would smile vaguely, as if uncertain whether he knew me or not. Robert sold me two raffle tickets, one to save endangered tigers and one to Save the Children, and gave me a rain forest poster, which I hung in my room. In spite of his forbidding eyebrows, Robert seemed the most friendly of the Harwoods, but he didn't ask me to come to tea. I was too young.

When it was wet, I liked to sit by my bedroom window, curled up in the armchair, watching the rain falling on the garden next door, making the leaves shine. I still got tired easily. I spent a lot of time dreaming.

It was on one of the wet days, just over a week later, that I first saw the face at the attic window.

2

There was something unnatural about it, and yet something familiar, too. It might almost have been a shadowed reflection of my own face. Since my illness, this was how I looked, pale and thin and nervous, with the peeping curiosity of someone newly out of danger. But its hair was dark, while mine is lank and pale. My eyes are blue. Its eyes looked like black holes in parchment. It seemed frightened. Always, when it caught sight of me at my window, it dodged back behind the curtain. Once I smiled and waved, but that seemed to frighten it even more. It was gone, quick as a ghost.

Could it be a ghost?

I told myself it was only some child visiting next door. Yet I never saw it in their garden, either with the Harwoods or by itself, nor in the street. Odd.

When the rain stopped, I hung about outside our house, bouncing a ball on the pavement, until I saw Christopher and Victoria coming out of their front door. I went to meet them.

"Hello," I said.

Neither of them looked pleased to see me.

"We're in a hurry," Victoria said abruptly, and would have walked past me but I got in her way. Curiosity gave me courage.

"I see you've got someone staying in your attic," I said brightly. "I wondered if whoever it is would like to play with me?"

"What are you talking about? There's nobody staying with us. You must be imagining things," she said, looking me straight in the eyes as she spoke. I was sure she was lying.

"There's lots of junk in our attic," Christopher told me. "Boxes piled up, old lampshades . . . It's easy to imagine things, you know." His voice was very reasonable. His face seemed innocent. I didn't believe him either. "It moved," I said.

Their eyes met above my head.

"It's difficult to see things clearly through glass," Christopher suggested. "What with reflections, leaves blowing about and —"

"And your own face!" Victoria cried triumphantly. "I bet that's what you saw, the reflection of your own face. Ever since you came, you've been spying on us. Whenever I look up, I see your face at the window, staring."

My cheeks burned. "I wasn't spying. I've been ill. I have to rest a lot. Auntie Amy put the armchair by the window in my room, so that I could look out and — and —"

"And watch us?"

"And watch the birds," I cried angrily.

"Ah, I see. You're an ornithologist," Christopher said, obviously not believing me.

For which I could hardly blame him. I had been watching *them*. Any spectacular bird, like a parrot, might have distracted me for a moment, but none had passed. There had only been sparrows and blackbirds and pigeons, ordinary birds like that, too familiar to compete with the Harwoods as an attraction.

I hated Christopher's superior smile. Auntie Amy told me he was supposed to be clever and was hoping to be a lawyer. I could imagine him in court, smooth and sneering, making you say things you didn't mean and then pointing out how stupid you were.

Victoria tugged his sleeve, wanting him to come with her, but he said, "Just a minute, Vicky. I've just remembered something I haven't done. I won't be long. You can plan what you're going to give us for supper tonight while you're waiting. Don't forget it's your turn. Perhaps Lesley can suggest something."

Again their eyes met above my head. Then he turned and ran back into the house.

To my surprise, Victoria did ask my advice. Their parents were away, she told me, and they were taking turns cooking.

"I didn't see why I should do it all, just because I'm a girl," she said. "Christopher tried to get out of it by saying he'd been left in charge, being the eldest. He'll be eighteen soon."

She talked quickly, her eyes moving from me to their house. She started asking me questions. What was my favorite thing to eat? Did I watch *Neighbors?* What was my school like?

"I don't start there until September," I reminded her.

"That's good," she said vaguely.

I don't think she'd heard a word I'd said. She seemed to be talking at random, while her mind was on something else. Her brother was gone quite a long time. When he came out of the house, he was breathless and flushed.

"Found it," he said, showing us the book in his hand, as if it were evidence. I saw that its title was *Gone to Earth.* Victoria smiled, and they went off together.

I stood looking after them, tossing the ball in my hand, trying to think. Then I ran back into our house and raced up to my room. I opened the window wide and stared across at the attic window next door. The face was not there. I sat in my chair and waited for it, but it did not come. As usual, the attic window was shut. Through the dusty glass, I could see vague shapes in the shadowy room. My sight is good. I knew they hadn't been there before. Somebody had piled things up into the rough semblance of a seated figure.

Christopher Harwood, I bet! Christopher racing up to the attic, while his sister kept me talking on the pavement below. What had he done with the child?

Auntie Amy was out shopping. If she'd been in, I think I'd have told her all about it. Perhaps not. As I walked slowly through the empty house, my imaginings became too dark and wild. I remembered the title of the book, *Gone to Earth*. I thought of murder and burial and kidnapping. I thought of a mad child locked away . . .

Auntie Amy was too old and gentle for such things. She wouldn't believe they could happen. Not next door. Not in a nice district like this. She'd think it was all my imagination. I'd heard what my mother told her before she left for Cairo.

"It'll do Lesley good to be quiet. She's become very nervous and fanciful since her illness. I've been worried about her."

14

They'd say I'd imagined the face, but I had not. I *had* seen it. And somehow I'd find it again.

At lunch, I asked my aunt if she had any binoculars I could borrow.

"We had some," she said. "Roy and I used to go to the races. He was very fond of racing. He once told me he'd have liked to be a jockey, but he grew too tall."

I was surprised. I could not imagine her going to the races or marrying a man who had wanted to be a jockey. It seemed too dashing a life for my quiet aunt. Perhaps she had changed when her husband died.

"Now where could I have put them?"she went on, frowning. "I haven't seen them for ages . . . Did I sell them? No. I remember now. I gave them to the church for their new roof." I must have looked puzzled, because she added, "They're always having rummage sales, dear, and I didn't have time to make any jam. So I'm afraid they're gone."

"It doesn't matter," I said, disappointed.

"I've got some opera glasses you can have. They aren't as strong, of course, but they're quite good ones. They're in the top drawer of that little chest. I came across them the other day."

They were old ones, gilt and mother-of-pearl, in a soft leather case. Small enough to fit in my pocket. Strong enough for my purpose.

"Can I really borrow them?" I asked, for they looked valuable.

"You can keep them, Lesley," she told me kindly. "I don't suppose I'll ever go to the opera again."

It seemed sad. She had so little fun. "I'll take you when I grow up," I promised.

She smiled. "I'll look forward to that. Thank you."

She didn't ask me what I wanted them for. My mother would have. Mum always wanted to know everything I did or thought. *Your letter came today, I wrote to her that night. It took over a week to get here. I'm glad you've settled in. I have, too. Ignore the complaints in my other letters, which I suppose you haven't gotten yet. Auntie Amy is very kind. She gave me her opera glasses today, and tomorrow I'm going to search for a small, secret bird. The Harwoods say it doesn't exist, but they're terrible liars.*

3

The houses on our street are all big and rather shabby, but not identical. Ours is at the end of a terrace of five Victorian houses, tall and narrow, each with a semibasement and a flight of steps up to the front door. Then there's a path through to the back.

The Harwoods' house stands on its own, with a garage on our side and a high wooden gate to its back garden on the other. It is wider, but not as tall as ours. My bedroom on the third floor is level with one of its attic windows, but it must have others. With my opera glasses in my pocket, I went out in search of them.

I didn't want the Harwoods to see me spying on them. I walked briskly past their house like someone minding her own business. The street was empty. I don't think anyone was watching me.

Their garden gate was set back from the sidewalk. It was locked. Glancing up at the side of the house, I saw a second attic window, high up in the otherwise blank wall. The sun glinted on the glass, hiding whatever lay behind it. I needed to be nearer.

The house on the other side was like ours, except it had five trash cans in the front garden, their lids numbered in white paint. I climbed the steps to the front door, took out my opera glasses, and looked through them. The attic window came sharply into view. I could see smears on the glass, chipped paint on the frame, shadows on the ceiling of the room behind. But no face.

These two attic windows were the only ones I could find, though I looked all round their house. Where could the child be?

For days I haunted the sidewalk outside, bouncing my ball or skipping with an old rope Auntie Amy had found for me. I felt like a fool, a girl of my age playing like a kid, but it gave me an excuse to be there.

"You again?" Victoria said, when she saw me there for the third time. "I thought you were supposed to rest."

"They say fresh air is good for me."

"Why not sit in a deck chair in your back garden? Wouldn't that be better for you than bouncing about with a skipping rope?"

"I'm supposed to have exercise too," I told her.

"You're overdoing it. Your face is bright red and you're puffing like a train. It can't be good for you. You'll probably drop dead any minute."

"I feel all right," I said.

She scowled. Then she shrugged and walked off.

"Thank you for your concern!" I called after her sweetly.

Twenty minutes later, Christopher and Robert came out of their house. I was sitting on our garden wall now, pretending to draw the house opposite. Christopher ignored me and said something to Robert that I couldn't hear. Robert came over. He didn't smile.

"Victoria's right. You're always hanging around. What for?" he asked.

"I'm drawing."

He glanced at my sketchbook and said coldly, "You certainly need practice."

"Yes," I admitted.

My reasonable answers seemed to annoy him. I thought for a minute he was going to snatch the sketchbook out of my hands and throw it at something. Me, probably. But then his brother called him and he ran off.

I watched them out of sight, waited five minutes in case they hadn't really gone, then went up to their front door and rang the bell. I could hear it ringing in the house, but nobody came. I hadn't expected anyone to. I knew that Mrs. Douglas, their cleaner, only came on Wednesdays, and today was Monday. The child wouldn't come. It would be frightened to hear the bell ringing in the empty house. It would be cowering somewhere. Or it might be locked in.

I looked through the windows of the ground floor. There were no net curtains and the glass was clean. I could see clearly that both rooms were empty. The one on the left of the front door was a sitting room, very tidy, with gold-framed pictures on the walls and Persian rugs on the floors. The one on the right must be where Mr. Harwood worked when he was at home. There was a desk with a computer on it, brown leather chairs, old and scuffed, and the walls were covered with bookshelves. It was neat and slightly dusty. Neither room looked as if it was used much.

The windows on the second floor were too high for me to see anything except the lampshades hanging from their ceilings. Nobody stood by them, gazing down at me. Nobody dodged behind the curtains.

If only I could get into their house. I tried to

climb their high garden gate, but it was made of stout wood, painted dark green, smooth and slippery. My fingers could not reach the top, even when I jumped.

"Stop that! What do you think you're doing?" Christopher shouted.

I swung round. The three of them had come back and were glaring at me. Victoria seemed almost pleased, as if she was glad I'd been found out.

"I told you she was up to something," she said.

"My b-ball," I stammered. "I was tossing it up and — and it went over your gate. I was trying to see where it had gone."

"You have to admire her," Robert said. "She has an excuse ready for every occasion."

"She's a nasty little liar," Victoria cried. She thrust her hand into my bulging jacket pocket before I could stop her, and brought out the ball. "What's this, then? And what's in your other pocket?" She reached out, but I slapped her hand away before she could find my opera glasses.

"Leave me alone!"

"Stop spying on us, then. We're sick of you," she said. "You're mad!"

"She's been ill, they say," Christopher said slowly, looking at me. "We ought to be sorry for her. Perhaps she suffers from delusions."

It shook me. Why did they hate me so? I pushed

past them and ran back to our house. I didn't want to see Auntie Amy. I didn't want to see anyone. I lay on my bed and cried.

"She's become very nervous and fanciful since her illness. I worry about her," my mother had said.

She shouldn't have gone off and left me, then.

I wasn't mad. I'd had a virus infection and turned yellow. It's true I'd had strange nightmares, but that had been the fever. The doctor had said so.

Delusions . . . I went over to my mirror to see if I looked sick and silly. My eyelids were puffy, but days of snooping in the sun had brought color to my thin cheeks. I no longer looked like a girl who saw shadows.

Had I really imagined it all? The sallow face with black eyes like holes, the way it dodged behind the curtain when it saw me, so terrified that the curtains shivered in sympathy — had it really only been the pile of cardboard boxes I could see now through my opera glasses? I didn't know.

There really was a child. I saw it that night. Something woke me, I don't know what. I got up and looked out of my window. I saw four shadowy figures running over the pale grass next door. One was tall, his fair hair white in the moonlight. The other two, a boy and a girl, were darker. The fourth

22

was small and thin and had hair as black and ragged as the clouds. They were all wearing pajamas, and their pale bare feet left dark prints on the silvered lawn. I flung open my window and cried out, "I can see you!" but they vanished behind some bushes.

I did not see them come back. I fell asleep in my chair, waiting for them, and when I woke, it was morning.

The next day, at three o'clock in the afternoon, Mrs. Harwood came back. I was sitting on our garden wall again, finishing my drawing of the house opposite, when a taxi drew up outside their gate. Mrs. Harwood got out of it, long legs and sensible shoes, long arms spilling out shopping bags and parcels onto the pavement.

I dropped my sketchbook onto the flower bed behind our wall and came over. "Can I help you carry anything in?" I asked, when she'd finished paying the driver.

"You absolute angel," she said, beaming at me and waving her hands in the air, perhaps to suggest wings. "Let me see, you're Lois, aren't you?"

"Lesley," I told her.

"Lesley, of course. Didn't I say Lesley? It's what I meant, but I'm in such a state, darling. All these parcels . . . I've been dropping them all over Victoria Station. Being a nuisance to everybody. Will you really help? Can you manage these? You're a pet, a positive lamb."

She loaded me up with parcels to my chin and, picking up the rest, led the way into the house.

"Throw them down anywhere," she told me. "In that corner will do. That's fine. Now come and have some tea. You'd like some tea, wouldn't you, Lesley?"

"Yes, thank you, Mrs. Harwood."

"Call me Kate," she said. "Come on. Let's see if there's some cake anywhere."

I was in at last. I glanced up the stairs hopefully, but no child ducked out of sight into the shadows. Then I followed Call-me-Kate into the kitchen.

"Christopher! Robert! Victoria!" she called loudly. "Look who I've brought you."

4

They stared. Victoria's hard brown eyes bulged with such fury that I half expected them to shoot out of her head like cannonballs. This was more than simple unfriendliness: war was declared. If their mother hadn't been there, I'd have been tempted to run.

"Come and sit down over here," she said kindly. "Mind that carton! Robert, put the kettle on, there's a pet. Vicky, see if you can find some cake. Otherwise, it'll have to be bread and jam."

I sat down obediently. While they were busy getting tea, I looked around me. If I'd been nervous before, it was nothing to what I felt now. Their kitchen was like something out of a nightmare. It was a large room, made small by the cardboard boxes piled up against the walls and the heaps of trash bags everywhere, tied up with string and labeled with the names of various charities. In the middle, there was a large pine table, littered with leaflets, dirty plates, a half-empty milk bottle, school books, a half-eaten loaf of brown bread in a scattering of crumbs, an open packet of butter covered with black specks, and a saucer of jam with two dead wasps in it. (What had they died of? I wondered. Poison?)

It was not this that upset me. Though Auntie Amy is tidy, my mother and I are not. I was used to chaos at home, though not on so large a scale. I knew that the black specks on the butter were probably only the crumbs of burnt toast, and the milk in the smeary bottle might be only a little sour.

What horrified me were the posters. They were pinned up all around the kitchen, on every cupboard, on every spare patch of wall. Wherever I looked, starving children with pitifully thin arms and legs and swollen bellies held out pleading hands. Boys, no older than I was, cradled machine guns to their narrow chests. In landscapes of dust and destruction, corpses lay in the sun, wrecked trucks rusted beside the bones of dead animals . . .

I felt sick and dizzy. I wanted to go home. I sat on the chair Call-me-Kate had given me and thought I was going to faint.

A hand touched my arm. Glancing up, I saw Robert watching me.

"Don't look at them if they make you feel bad. We've gotten used to them. After a time, you don't see them anymore." He spoke in a whisper, but his mother heard him.

"Are you talking about the posters?" she asked. "We keep them here to remind ourselves. It's so easy to forget the hunger and pain of others when it's hidden away. It's up to us who are lucky to share our good fortune, don't you think?"

I nodded. It was true. Nobody could deny it. And yet . . . in their kitchen? How could they eat in here? How could they bear it?

Victoria slapped a plate with a slice of cake on it onto the table in front of me so hard that I thought the plate would crack. Glancing up at her face, I saw it wore an expression of misery and resentment. For once I didn't think it was directed at me. It was her mother she was looking at from beneath her lashes.

Suddenly I felt sorry for her. I remembered how often I'd seen her carrying great bundles of clothes to the charity shop or standing cheerfully in the rain, shaking a box at passing crowds. She did her share willingly. They all did. They didn't need posters to remind them.

I couldn't touch my cake. It would've choked me. When I thought nobody was looking, I broke off small pieces and pushed them into the pockets of my jeans. (For weeks afterward, even after they'd been washed, I kept finding soggy crumbs.)

Robert was sitting next to me. Before I'd gotten rid of more than half of my cake in this way, he caught me at it and whispered angrily, "If you don't want it, give it to me. Only don't let Mum see."

His plate was empty. So were Christopher's and Victoria's. Not a crumb left. As clean as if they'd licked them. The posters hadn't put them off. "After a while, you don't see them," Robert had said.

I passed him the remainder of my cake under the table. He didn't put it on his plate, but held it in his hand below the table. I glanced at his mother to see if she'd noticed, but she was talking to Christopher. When I looked back at Robert, the cake was gone. Vanished. I thought he must've crammed it into his mouth and swallowed it greedily in a single gulp. I was stupid. I never thought of the child in the attic.

When tea was over, Call-me-Kate said, "Why don't you show Lesley your room, Vicky?"

Vicky got sulkily to her feet. "Then Christopher and Robert can clean up," she said, making it plain that entertaining me was a chore on this level. She held the kitchen door open for me, turned round to the others, and said urgently, "Don't start until I come back, will you? I won't be long."

"Start what?" her mother asked, but Victoria shut the kitchen door on her without answering.

Then she turned to me.

"I suppose you think you're clever, wheedling your way in," she said. "I hope you're satisfied, because you've seen all you're going to see. I'm not taking you up to my room. I'm fussy whom I invite. You can go straight out the front door and stay out. We don't want you. None of us do. Mum only asked you to tea because she's sorry for you. Do you understand?"

Although her words were rude, she spoke them quietly, without any venom. I thought her attention was not on me, but on the room we'd just left. She was longing to go back. She was afraid of missing something.

Her rudeness released me from embarrassment. Polite people make me shy, because I'm afraid of making mistakes, but I felt I could hardly behave worse than Victoria did.

"What about the child you're hiding?" I asked. "Does your mother know about it?"

"You're mad! What child? There isn't any child. How many times do I have to tell you?"

"I saw it last night," I said.

"You were dreaming!" she said and, taking me

roughly by the arm, pushed me out of the front door and shut it in my face.

I stared at it furiously for a moment, then turned and ran back to my aunt's house. I went in the back way, quietly. Auntie Amy was having friends to tea today. She'd invited me to join them — they were having two sorts of cream cake, chocolate and vanilla, and she'd made some cucumber sandwiches, my favorites. I hesitated, trying to think of an excuse, and she said quickly, "Don't worry if you're not feeling up to it, Lesley. I'll leave you a tray in the kitchen, then you can join us or not, as you wish."

She was very kind, but I didn't want to see her now. I wanted to know what was going on next door. I wanted to see the face again. I was worried now. Had I been dreaming?

Our back garden was a wild place, overgrown with ivy, full of weeds and strangling trees. Auntie Amy didn't like eating outdoors because of wasps and gnats. She was an indoor person, pale as a mushroom. They'd be having their tea in the sitting room at the front, drinking from delicate china laid out on small, wobbly, long-legged tables, easy to knock over. I'd have the garden to myself.

I could not see the Harwoods' attic window clearly from here. The gap between our houses was in shadow. I walked through the long, browning grass to where I'd left the deck chair yesterday, half hidden behind an evergreen shrub. The canvas seat was cool, still slightly damp from last night's dew. I sat down and looked up at the back of their house, not expecting to see anything. The top-floor windows were opaque with reflected sunlight. The garden wall was too high for me to see the ground-floor windows, but one of them must have been open, because I heard, quite clearly, Victoria shouting.

Her voice was harsh, choked with tears. "I hate you! You're a hypocrite! A stinking hypocrite! After all you've said, all these years . . . I thought you meant it. I believed you. And all the time — I hate you! You know what'll happen. They'll send him back and he'll be killed. Don't you care?"

Her mother said something, but I could not make out the words because Victoria kept shouting, and now Robert joined in, saying something about "deceiving us."

I got up from my deck chair, went over to the garden wall, and climbed up the stout old trellis till I could just see over the top, through a screen of leaves. They were in their sitting room. I could see them dimly through the sunlit glass, dark shadows that reflected the green of the garden. They were all shouting now. I heard Call-me-Kate say loudly, "Now that's enough!" Then they moved away and

31

I heard a door slam. They had gone to continue their quarrel elsewhere.

I hadn't been the only listener. A sudden scraping noise made me glance up into the gap between our two houses. The attic window was wide open, and a small boy was crouching on the sill with his back to me. I put my hand over my mouth to stop myself from crying out and startling him. Slowly he lowered himself until he was hanging by his hands over the flat garage roof some nine feet below. Then he let himself drop.

5

The boy landed with a thud, rolled over twice, and was on his feet again, staggering a little. He looked around, then tiptoed toward the front of the garage. He must have seen something in the street that alarmed him, because he retreated hastily. Now he came and peered down into the gardens. He gave no sign of having noticed me behind my screen of leaves. Crouching on the edge, he looked doubtfully at the ground below.

I knew that face.

It was the face I'd been looking for, the face I'd only seen before through the dusty glass of the attic window. I knew those watchful black eyes, that sallow skin and nervous mouth.

Seeing it sharp and clear in the afternoon sunlight, I knew he was a boy, even though he was dressed much as I was. His jet-black hair hung lankly below his ears, like mine, except that mine is fair. Like me, he wore a T-shirt far too large for him, which drooped in folds from his bony shoulders. His denim trousers were bunched round his narrow waist, held up by a leather belt. Both his hair and his trousers looked as if they'd been cut short with a pair of blunt scissors.

He turned his head and stared toward our wall. I froze. I was afraid that if he saw me through the leaves, he might vanish again, wipe himself out with a curtain of sunlight and disappear. Victoria's repeated denials of his existence had upset me. I was no longer certain that he was real.

But he was no airy figment of my imagination. Small as he was, when he jumped, he landed heavily, falling forward onto his hands and knees. He got to his feet slowly, his face twisted with pain. When he came toward the wall, he was limping badly.

Behind him, a door opened and Robert came out of the house.

The boy must have heard him. He didn't waste time looking over his shoulder, but broke into a hobbling run and leapt for the wall. He was so near me that when his fingers slipped, I was able to reach out from the leaves that hid me and grab hold of his wrist.

He cried out in fright and tried to pull away.

"I'm your friend! I'll help you! Quick!" I whispered.

I attempted to drag him up onto the wall, but he hung from my hand and made no effort to help himself. Then Robert was on him, catching him round the legs.

"Let him go!" I cried, before I realized that far from pulling him down, Robert was lifting him up.

"Hurry, before someone sees us," he said, and gave the boy such a strong shove that he shot over the wall and landed on top of me, knocking me off the trellis so that we tumbled together into the lavender bush below.

By the time we had disentangled ourselves, Robert too was over the wall and urging us to our feet.

"Quick! Get him out of sight! Where are you going to put him?"

"Who, me?" I asked stupidly.

"Yes, you," he replied impatiently. "Who else? You said you'd help him. I heard you. Besides there's nobody else. We can't do any more, now that Mum's ratted on us. Where's your aunt?"

"She's in the front, having tea with some friends. Do you want me to fetch her?"

"No! Are you mad? She mustn't know. You mustn't tell her about him. You mustn't tell anybody, do you understand?"

The boy had been standing limply between us, like a puppet waiting for us to jerk him into life.

Now he looked at me. His eyes were fixed and staring. I wondered if he was ill. Then I heard him speak for the first time. His voice was husky and foreign-sounding.

"Not tell," he said. "Pliss. They kill me. You not tell."

"It's all right. She won't tell," Robert told him, "she's going to hide you. You'll soon be safe again." He turned to me and added, "Where's he to go? Have you decided?"

"I don't know. I haven't thought —"

"Oh, wake up! What's the matter with you? Where can we go? What's through that door?"

"The kitchen."

"See if it's empty. We can't stay out here."

There was nobody in the kitchen. I held the door open and let them in. I saw the boy's eyes go to the tray my aunt had left on the table for me, with a glass waiting to be filled with milk and plates of sandwiches and cake covered with plastic wrap.

"Are you hungry?" I asked.

Before he had time to answer, Robert said quickly, "Not now, for heaven's sake! Your aunt could come along at any minute to fetch something. You need somewhere safe. Haven't you an attic?"

"I suppose so. I don't know how you get up

36

there. But there are empty rooms on the third floor. There's one leading off mine that might do. It's not very big, but there's a bed in it. It used to be a dressing room or something. Nobody ever goes there. I have the third floor all to myself."

"Good," Robert said. "Now, you've got to get him up there without anyone seeing. How are you going to do that?"

"Aren't you going to help?"

"I have to get back —" he began, then looked at me and shrugged. "Oh, all right. Where does this door lead?"

"Into the hall."

"Open it quietly and see if the way is clear. We'll keep out of sight."

The hall was patterned with shadows. Light came through the stained-glass panel in the front door and painted red flowers and green leaves on the polished wooden floor. It was very quiet.

Robert came and peered over my shoulder. "Are they in this room here?"

"No, that's the dining room. The sitting room's the next one."

"It's easy, then. You don't even have to pass it to reach the stairs. You go ahead, and if there's nobody coming down —"

"There won't be. I told you. They're having tea in the front room."

37

"Somebody might've gone up to the bathroom and come out just as you're passing. You must try and think of things like that. It's no good if you're going to be careless. I can't be with you all the time. Here, better take this tray up with you, if she left it for you. He's always hungry and I didn't have time to give him our cake." He handed me the tray and pushed me gently through the open door. "If it's all right, beckon and I'll send him to you," he said.

"Aren't you coming?"

"I told you. I must get back or Mum will get suspicious. I'll try to come later. Or I'll send Victoria round. Yes, that'll be best. She'll tell you everything. Go on, now."

"But —"

"Don't worry. Once you've gotten him safely upstairs, you'll be all right. He's very quick and quiet. He won't give you away."

"But you haven't told me —"

"Go on!"

He pushed me forward. There were a hundred things I wanted to ask him, but there wasn't time. I was on my way. My feet in their soft shoes seemed to thunder on the polished wood. When I reached the banister and looked up, I saw the stairs curving out of sight. We always left the bathroom door ajar when it was empty, but I couldn't see it from here.

I'd better check. "It's no good if you're going to be careless," Robert had said. I started up the stairs.

Perhaps Robert had never meant to wait for me to beckon. Perhaps the boy himself thought I was deserting him. I was only on the fifth step when he slipped past me, as silent as a shadow, and joined the other shadows on the landing above. Downstairs I heard the kitchen door shut softly. Robert had gone.

I wondered uneasily what I had let into the house.

6

I sat in my chair and stared at him. So this was the face I'd once thought was a dark reflection of my own. The dusty glass of the attic window had flattered it. Now that it was in my own room, stuffing itself with the sandwiches and cake that my aunt had left out for me, it turned out to be the face of a greedy little boy. I had held out the two plates to him politely, expecting him to choose. Instead he'd taken them both into his small hands, leaving me nothing.

Victoria was right: I must be mad.

I liked my aunt. How could I have done this to her? I knew nothing of the boy. He might be a criminal. He might get up in the night while I slept and go rummaging through her house to see what he could steal. He might invade her workroom and trample on the expensive silks and satins with his dirty bare feet. He might sneer at the china babies that crowded every mantelpiece in every room: the small girls holding kittens or flowers, the small boys with puppies. "My children," she'd called them once, with a self-mocking smile, adding, "My only children until you came, Lesley."

"I can only stay till Mum comes back," I'd reminded her quickly. This was before I'd gotten my first letter from Cairo, and I was anxious, even though my mother had already telephoned to say she'd arrived safely. I didn't want Auntie Amy to think of me as *her* child. I was my mother's.

Now my aunt had another child in her house, a secret child. Somehow I didn't think she would like him as much as her china children. There was a wild look about him. He didn't look like the sort of boy you could put on the mantelpiece and keep in order with a featherduster.

I watched him, trying to recapture the warmth I'd felt for him when I'd cried, "I'm your friend. I'll help you."

He was sitting cross-legged on my bed, with his dirty bare feet on my white coverlet, cramming the last slice of cake into his mouth with both hands, and dropping crumbs everywhere like brown snow. He didn't really look like me at all. It was only that we were both thin and sickly. He was smaller and much younger than I was, no more than seven or eight years old, a mere kid. His shaggy black hair was uncombed, and his skin had a yellowish tinge. His black eyes still looked frightened. Every time I moved in my chair, he jumped and shook. He was so frail, I felt I could blow him away. I was tempted to try.

I ought to have felt sorry for him. I couldn't understand myself. Surely I wasn't so mean that I was cross with him because he'd eaten all my cake?

"What's your name?" I asked him.

He stared at me and didn't answer.

I repeated the question, speaking slowly and clearly, but he spread his hands helplessly.

"What are you called?" I tried.

"Cold?" He shook his head. "Not cold. Hanku."

"You're not called Hanku?" I asked, puzzled. "What are you called, then?"

He spread his hands again and said something in a foreign language. Not French, I thought. We were doing French at school, and it didn't sound the same at all. Anyway, my French is poor, so I didn't attempt it. Instead I tried Tarzan language. Tapping myself on the chest, I said, "Me Lesley."

I'd never seen him smile before. It changed his face. You'd never mistake him for a ghost now. Ghosts don't smile, at least none I'd ever heard of do. Skulls grin, of course, but that's not the same. He must have seen the Tarzan films, for he beat his thin chest with both hands, like a gorilla, and said, "Me Erri."

"Erri?"

He nodded and then, pointing at me, said, "Lesley."

At least we had introduced ourselves. We didn't get much further. Tarzan language is limited. I could point to things and tell Erri what they were called in English, and he would say a foreign word and shake his head critically when I tried to repeat it. Whenever I asked him something that I really wanted to know, like "Where have you come from? Why are you so frightened? Who is trying to kill you?" all I got in reply was the spread hands and bewildered shrug.

I was soon bored with it, and I imagine he was too. In the silences when I couldn't think of anything to say, he stared at me nervously, as if he didn't know what I was going to do next. I kept looking at my clock and wondering if it had stopped. I longed for Robert or even Victoria to come.

At any moment, Auntie Amy's friends would leave, and she would wonder where I was. Often, being tired, she would just call up the stairs. Sometimes she came up to my room. Though she always knocked on my door, it wasn't safe to let the boy stay here. I must settle him into the room next door. There was a bed for him to sit on, though it had no pillows or blankets. There was a window that looked out at the front, though it had no view, except for the fir tree that grew too close to the house and shut out the light. It was a small, bare, dark room and I didn't think he'd like it. Too bad.

He followed me when I beckoned and sat down obediently on the narrow bed. He didn't say anything. I fetched him one of my pillows and a blanket from one of the spare bedrooms. I couldn't let him have my radio to play in a room that was supposed to be empty, and books in English would be no use to him. There was nothing for him to do. At least in the Harwoods' attic, he'd been able to look out of the window.

I felt sorry for him now. He looked so small and sad, like a prisoner in a cell.

"I'm going to get Robert and Victoria from next door," I told him, slowly and clearly. "They're your friends, aren't they? Erri stay here. Do you understand?"

He looked frightened. "Not go," he said, and caught hold of my arm. His hand was so thin and small, it was like a grasshopper trying to stop me. I had to go. I needed help.

I pulled away. "Erri stay here. Not make noise. Lesley lock door so Erri is safe —"

He understood that all right and was on his feet,

44

trying to race me to the door, but I was through it first and shut it in his face and turned the key. Then I stood listening.

He shook the handle. I was afraid he'd hammer on the door and start screaming, but he didn't. After a while, he stopped shaking the handle and there was silence.

I couldn't leave him locked in. I couldn't leave him in that small, dark room in an unfamiliar house, alone with his nightmares. I unlocked the door again and went back into the room.

He was standing by the window with his back to me. I think he'd been trying to open it. He turned round and looked at me.

"I'm afraid it won't open. I think the paint has stuck," I told him, going over. I raised my hands to the window, and he flinched away from me, putting an arm up to protect his head. There were fading bruises on his sallow skin.

"Erri, I wasn't going to hit you! It's all right. I'm your friend. I won't hurt you. I was just going to try the window. I'm sorry I locked you in. I just thought you'd be safer —" This wasn't true. I hadn't liked the thought of leaving the house open to him while I was gone. I was afraid he'd steal things. "Look, you have the key," I said, handing it to him.

I don't know if he understood what I said, but when I put the key in his hand, his face lightened.

It was better than words. He thought I trusted him, so he was prepared to trust me a little.

"I'm going now. When I go, you, Erri, lock door behind me. So nobody can come in, understand?"

He nodded.

I shut his door behind me and heard the key turn. Then I crossed to my own door and took the key out of the lock. The only way out of his room was through mine — that was why I'd chosen it for him. There were plenty of other empty rooms in my aunt's house, but I'd wanted him under my eye. I could lock him in without his knowing — unless he came through my room and tried this door.

If he found it locked, he'd never trust me again.

I was still hesitating when the doorbell rang. I went racing down the stairs, but I had two flights to do, and my aunt got there before me.

I heard Victoria say in her loud, clear voice, "Lesley said we could come over. Did she tell you?"

7

He must have heard our footsteps. The Harwoods are heavy on their feet, not like Erri and me, who are both on the silent side. They came clattering into my bedroom. Heaven knows what Erri thought — that I had betrayed him, perhaps, that I'd brought in his enemies, whoever they were. I knocked on his door and called softly, "Erri, it's me. Lesley. Let me in."

Silence.

"Don't tell me you've lost him already," Victoria said in disgust. "Why did you give him the key? You must be mad. You should've locked him in, not let him lock us out. He's probably escaped through the window."

"I thought we were supposed to be helping him, not imprisoning him," I said hotly.

"Comes to the same thing. He's only a kid.

He can't manage without our help. What could he do?"

"Who is he? What's he afraid of?"

"Being sent back," she muttered, and pushed me away from the door. "Erri, it's me. Vicky. Your friend."

Silence. I could not help being glad that he would not open the door for her, either.

"Could he have gotten out of the window?" Robert asked me.

"No. It won't open. I tried it."

"He could've broken the glass," Victoria pointed out. "Where is this window? Over the garage roof, I suppose?"

"No. It's at the front of the house."

"Not behind that great fir tree?"

I was silent.

"Then he's gone," she said. "I bet he can climb like a cat."

Robert was listening at the door, his ear pressed against the wooden panel. He straightened up and said loudly, "Well, if he's gone, he's gone. We might as well eat the chocolate we brought for him. Poor Erri, he loved *chocolate*. Especially MILK CHOCOLATE."

We all waited, watching the door. There was the sound of the key being turned in the lock. Then the door opened and Erri stood there, rubbing his eyes as if he'd just woken up from a deep sleep. Perhaps he had, but somehow I doubted it. He smiled slyly when Robert handed him the chocolate and said, "Hanku."

" 'Thank you,' Erri, not 'hanku,' " Victoria said. She pushed past him and looked round the small room, first at the unbroken window with the fir tree pressing outside, then at the narrow bed with its crumpled blanket and single pillow, the gray carpet on the floor, the bare walls. "What a horrible little room. Couldn't you do better for him than this?" she demanded. "It's like a prison cell."

"At least it's a proper room, not an attic."

"Our attic is ten times nicer than this," she told me scornfully. "I wouldn't mind moving up there myself. What's he supposed to do in here, poor little devil? You might've given him something to play with."

"I haven't any toys. Mum burned them when I was ill."

"What!"

"In case they were infectious," I explained, glad to have startled her. "The doctor said later that it wasn't necessary. They could've been fumigated. But she was afraid. She said she felt happier knowing they'd been burned."

"Even your old teddy?" Robert asked. "Poor old you. What did you have, the plague?"

49

"Hepatitis. How did you know I had an old teddy?"

"Everyone has an old teddy. Except, of course, people whose mothers burn them. Perhaps she thought it was a sort of sacrifice to the gods. You know the sort of thing — 'let Lesley recover and you can have all her toys to play with in heaven.' "

I laughed. It annoyed Victoria.

"We're just wasting time," she said tartly. "You can tell us all about your illness some other day, if you must. And I didn't mean that sort of toy. I meant something to do. Don't you have any felt pens or paints? A pencil and a few sheets of paper would be better than nothing. Some Legos, or a jigsaw. He'll go mad in here without anything to do."

"I thought you'd come any minute. I didn't think you'd be so long," I said defensively. "Of course I'd have given him something . . ."

The boy was sitting on his bed. He had broken the bar of chocolate into separate squares and was eating them slowly, with relish, not the way he'd gobbled the cake. Perhaps he felt safer now, with his old friends in the room. He glanced up and, seeing that I was looking at him, picked up a square of chocolate and held it out to me on the palm of his hand, like someone feeding a horse that might bite.

"Choclat?" he asked.

"Why, thank you, Erri," I said, touched.

"I like that! We bring the chocolate and she *eats* it," Victoria complained. "He doesn't think of offering it to us, not that I'd have accepted it. *We* haven't been starved —"

"He probably thinks Lesley has. She's as thin as he is. Stop getting at her, Vicky. We're on the same side." He turned to me. "What time do you have supper?" he asked.

"Half-past seven."

"We'd better get started. Give Erri some drawing things and we'll go into your room. It's more comfortable. You know, you'll have to get him a couple of chairs and a small table in here."

I stared at them. "But — but how long's he going to stay?"

"I don't know. A few weeks, perhaps," Victoria said carelessly.

"Until we've thought of something," Robert explained. "It's not easy. In fact, it's an awful mess, now that Mum's ratted on us. To be honest, I've no idea, not a single one. We're hoping that Christopher will come up with something."

I was appalled. What had I gotten myself into? At the worst, I'd thought I'd only have to hide the boy for a few hours — no, to be honest, I hadn't

51

thought at all. Things had happened too quickly. I'd been pushed into it. Erri had nothing to do with me.

"I can't keep him that long! My aunt's bound to find out. Who is he? Hasn't he got a —"

"Not in front of the children," Victoria interrupted quickly. "We think Jug-Ears over there understands more than he lets on. Yes, we're talking about you, Erri," she said to the boy, who was watching us intently. "We're saying what a clever little beggar you are. Now, kind Lesley is going to give you some paper and a pencil, and we want you to draw us a picture, while we go into her room and talk for a bit."

It was impossible to tell how much, if anything, he understood. He tried to follow us into my bedroom, but Victoria pushed him firmly back and I gave him my sketchbook and a box of felt pens. He turned the pages and, coming across my drawing of the house across the road, sniffed very loudly. All right, it wasn't a very good drawing, but one can't be good at everything.

"See if you can do better," I told him.

He caught hold of my arm, looking up at me anxiously. "Not go!" he said.

"Only into the next room. Look, I'll leave the door open. Is that all right now?"

"You have to be firm with him," Victoria said.

"You'll never manage if you let him have his own way. Erri, you stay here. Sit on bed. Draw picture. We come back soon."

She shut the door on him. "That's the way to handle him," she told me.

She sat on the foot of my bed, while I curled up on my remaining pillow. Robert turned the armchair away from the window so that he was facing us. We all glanced at Erri's closed door as if expecting it to open, but it remained shut.

"Now I suppose you want to know all about him," Victoria said. "We can't tell you much. His name is Erri, and he's an illegal immigrant. That's really all we know."

8

I knew what illegal immigrants were; at least I thought I did. They were people who'd sneaked into this country when they'd no right to be here. Not genuine refugees, not simple vacationers who came and spent their money and returned home, but people who hid under the floorboards of trucks or arrived in overcrowded boats in the middle of the night. It's true I didn't read newspapers much, but you couldn't watch television as often as Auntie Amy and I did without picking some things up.

It often puzzled me why they came, when it was so dangerous. Sometimes they died on the way. Their rickety boats sank or they suffocated in their hiding places, and it'd be in the news. I hated the news. It was so depressing. I tried not to watch when Auntie Amy switched it on.

"I suppose you think they should all be sent back?" Victoria asked.

I tried to remember what Auntie Amy had said about them, but she was so quiet. She used to watch the news in silence, occasionally sighing. "I don't know enough about it," I said.

"Well, I suppose it's something that you recognize that." Victoria sounded annoyed that I hadn't said the wrong thing, so that she could sneer at me and set me straight. But I hadn't known which was wrong or right. I hadn't listened to the arguments.

"What about Erri? Do you think he should be sent back?" she demanded, in that aggressive way of hers.

I thought of Erri clutching my arm. I thought of the terror in his face when he begged, "Not tell, not tell!"

"No," I said, "not Erri."

He was different. I knew him. I tried to imagine him flattened beneath the floorboards of a truck, lying in the rattling dark, with the sickening smell of gasoline and the exhaust fumes choking him. Or tossed in a boat too fragile for the fierce sea.

"What about his parents?" I asked.

"He says his mother's dead. As for his father, he just shrugs. We don't even know what country he comes from," Robert told me. "Don't think we haven't asked him."

"He knows what 'where' means," Victoria said. "Say 'Erri, where's the pencil,' and he'll find it and give it to you. But say 'Erri, where are you from? Where's your home?' and just see how blank he looks."

"Not blank, frightened," Robert said. "He doesn't want to remember."

He must have been desperate to leave his own country and come here, I thought. They all must be, or why do they do it, at such a risk?

"How did you find him?" I asked. "Did he come to you for help?"

It was a long story, they said, settling themselves comfortably, seeming pleased enough to tell me now. They told it in turns, one taking over when the other ran out of breath. Victoria started. I hadn't liked her. I'd thought she was arrogant and bossy, altogether nasty, in fact. But as she talked, I began to get a different picture.

It had happened by chance. They hadn't been looking for trouble. Their parents were going off on vacation for ten days, leaving them in charge of the house for the first time. They were delighted, though they tried not to show it. They planned to have parties, to invite their friends from school to stay —

"The last thing we wanted was to be landed with

a poor little victim," Victoria said. "We've had enough of charity all our lives. You can't imagine how sick you get of it. Mum's always been into good works. Mrs. Wonderful, that's how she sees herself, Saint Kate, mother of all the world. And she expects us to live up to her. I longed to be able to spend my pocket money on myself for a change, to buy silly little things without feeling guilty, bracelets and false eyelashes and pink leggings, the sorts of things my friends have. I don't mind helping with rummage sales and shaking collection boxes. I quite enjoy it, in fact. I want to help. But not all the time. Not every stinking day —"

She broke off suddenly and asked, "Why do you think I've been horrid to you?"

"I don't know," I said, surprised. "I thought you just didn't like my face or the way I talk or something."

She waved her hand as if brushing away unimportant details. "It was because of Mum, of course. You'd no sooner arrived next door than she was telling us that we must be kind to you because you'd been terribly ill, and you had no friends and your mother had left you —"

"That's not true!" I cried angrily. "At least, not the way you make it sound. Mum wanted to take me with her, but the doctors advised against it, and I've plenty of friends, only they're down in Devon, and —"

"I know, I know, calm down! But it's the way I heard it. It was ghastly, like having a lame duck move in next door. 'You can be her friend, Vicky,' she said. 'You're much the same age.' Much the same age! I'm three years older than you, near enough. She didn't ask the boys, oh no, just me because I'm a girl. It's hardly surprising I wanted to spit whenever I saw you. Another poor thing to be sorry for, always hanging about and staring at me reproachfully."

"I'm not a lame duck," I told her coldly, "and I wasn't even poor until Robert made me buy all those raffle tickets."

Robert laughed. "Victoria's just wasting time. You don't want to know about her feelings," he said. "You want to know how we met Erri. I'd better tell the rest of it."

It wouldn't have happened, he told me, if Christopher hadn't recently passed his driving test. He'd passed it the first time, no trouble. He'd always been mad about cars, in spite of their mother wanting them to ride bicycles because it was better for the environment. Chris had offered to drive his parents to Heathrow in return for being allowed to use the car while they were away. Robert had insisted on coming too.

"I love airports," he said, "especially now that they have those soldiers prowling about with their sinister black guns, like on the television. I wanted to see them. Who knows, they might have shot somebody before my eyes. High drama. Vicky didn't want to be left out, so we all went, though it was rather a squash in the back."

They were in a holiday mood. They must've looked too happy. It made their mother suspicious.

"You will be good when we're away, won't you?" she said. "You won't forget to collect for the Red Cross tomorrow."

"All right, all right, we won't forget," they assured her hastily. "You wrote it all down for us, remember? You'd better hurry or you'll miss your plane."

She'd looked hurt then, as if she knew they could hardly wait for her to go, so they'd hugged her and told her sweet lies about missing her.

"It's not that we don't love her, but you know how mothers are, always fussing and getting at you," Robert said. "We just wanted a bit of peace."

They'd waved their parents goodbye and watched them disappear into the departure lounge. Their sense of freedom went to their heads. Victoria began hopping about and crowing, and Christopher got cross with her. He was easily embarrassed, Robert said, now that he was almost grown up.

There was some sort of commotion going on around the exit. Robert looked through the glass doors and saw a group of people standing outside carrying banners with something written on them. He was too far away to read them clearly, all except the nearest, which said in large letters: TO SEND THEM BACK IS MURDER.

Policemen were pushing them away, making a line with linked arms to hold them back from another, smaller group that had just come off a bus nearby. This second group was accompanied by three official-looking men with clipboards and papers, one of whom was trying to count them and getting annoyed when the other two began hustling them toward one of the entrances, without allowing him time to finish.

Suddenly the banner-bearers surged forward, breaking through the police line, and for a moment the two groups mingled. To Robert's surprise, they didn't fight each other. In fact it looked to him as if the banner-bearers were trying to help the bus party get away. As he watched, fascinated, a few of them evaded the officials and pushed their way through the exit doors into the airport terminal, forcing their way through the people who were trying to get out.

Two soldiers on guard, noticing the disturbance, started moving toward them, holding their black guns in their hands. Their eyes were hard and bright. Robert felt his heart jump with excitement as he stared from the soldiers to the men who had pushed their way in. They didn't look like terrorists to him. They looked bewildered, frightened, and very tired. Their clothes were crumpled and stained, and one of them, an old man, was crying.

Robert opened his mouth, but before he could say anything, a small figure suddenly slipped out from behind a luggage cart and fell at Victoria's feet. Thin hands clutched her skirt, pleading black eyes stared up into hers.

"Not tell! Pliss, not tell," the boy cried. "They kill —"

Without taking time to think, without even looking up to see where the soldiers were or if either of them had noticed, Victoria threw the anorak she was carrying over the boy's shoulders and put up the hood to hide his ragged black hair. It was her new anorak, a glossy scarlet one with pale green and pink stripes on the arms, very conspicuous, and much too big for him. Robert noticed with alarm how odd he looked in it, with his terrified face framed by the hood at one end, and his thin dirty legs and bare feet at the other. Quickly, Robert picked him up and held him, hiding the boy's face against his shoulder.

"Keep close in front of me," he whispered to Victoria, "so that his feet won't show. That's right —"

"What are you doing? Have you gone mad?" Christopher demanded. "Who is that boy?"

They told him to shut up and come with them. "Do you want to get us into trouble? Come on, keep talking cheerfully. We've got to look natural," Robert said and, raising his voice, added loudly, "Where've Mum and Dad gone? They're always vanishing. We'd better go and look for them, I suppose."

They walked slowly away, with Christopher following, muttering under his breath, "You're mad! It's not a game, you know. Those are real guns. You could get us shot —"

"Are they looking this way?" Robert asked.

"They're checking all around — oh, they've caught one. And another. Who is that boy? What are you doing with him?"

"Trying to smuggle him out of here," Victoria told him breathlessly. "Mum would want us to help him, you know she would. She'd never hand him over to them. He's trembling, Chris. He's terrified.

Let's take him home and hide him until she gets back. She'll know what to do."

"That's what I thought then," Victoria broke in, her voice shaking. "I thought she'd be pleased. I thought she'd be proud of us!"

"Wasn't she?" I asked. I'd have been proud of them.

"The heck she was!" Victoria said.

9

Robert had said that they loved their mother. That he did, I could easily believe. He had a warm heart. The more I knew him, the more I liked him. For one thing, I thought he liked me, and I always find that an endearing quality in people. I was beginning to consider his heavy black eyebrows rather attractive. But Victoria, who looked like a rosy apple, was sharp and sour and full of hate.

"I used to believe in her," she said. "Oh, I joked about her, calling her Mrs. Wonderful and Mrs. Bleeding Heart, but I secretly thought she really was something special. I admired her, can you believe it? I felt it was my fault that I resented having to give away my pocket money and hated those terrible posters and was bored stiff by all the charity concerts. I thought I must have a nasty, mean nature, and wished I was more like her. I must've been mad! She's a cheat! A filthy humbug. 'Oh those poor, poor people,' she'd say, and I'll swear there were tears in her eyes. Crocodile! She pretends to be selfless and sympathetic — and what happens when we bring one of those poor, poor people home?"

She paused for breath, or perhaps for an answer.

"Wasn't she pleased?" I asked, only to prompt her, not because I was in any doubt. There was no need for her to raise her eyes to the ceiling and sigh heavily, in that insulting way.

"No, she wasn't pleased," she said with exaggerated patience. "She blew her top, she exploded, she screamed at us! She said we must've been mad. She said we'd get Dad into trouble —"

"Your father? Why? Did you get him to help with Erri?"

"No, of course he didn't help us. How could he? He wasn't there."

"Dad's not back," Robert explained. "He had to go straight to Brussels to join his boss. He's in the Civil Service and works for the government, you see. That's why Mum was so worried. She said he couldn't afford the scandal. The opposition would get hold of it and play it up. You know the sort of thing — 'Cabinet Minister's staff flouts government policy. Illegal immigrant hidden in attic.' She said it could ruin his career. Even though he doesn't know anything about it, they'd always say he must've known."

"At worst he'd only lose his job," Victoria said scornfully.

I stared at her. My mother was terrified of losing her job. She said once — not to me, she thought I was asleep — but to a friend of hers: "I don't know what I'd do. Supposing I couldn't get another one? I don't see how people manage on welfare. I can hardly manage as it is."

Victoria must have seen my astonishment because she explained, "They wouldn't shoot him, would they? But that's what they'll do to Erri if he's sent back."

"What!"

"Shoot him!" she cried impatiently.

"Who will?"

"How should I know? I don't know where he comes from or which side he's on. Does it matter? Don't you ever watch the news? There're wars all over the place. You can take your choice of countries. All I know is that he said they'd kill him if he was sent back."

"It may not be true, of course," Robert said, "but it's obvious he believes it, poor little beggar. He was terrified. Even Chris was won over when he saw him. Until then he'd been saying we were mad, just like Mum, but when he saw Erri, when he saw the way he trembled and the expression in his eyes — well, he didn't say any more about giving him up to the authorities."

"What did your mother say when she saw Erri? Wasn't she sorry for him?"

"She hasn't seen him," Victoria said. "I wasn't going to tell her where he was — I didn't trust her, not after what she'd said — but Chris gave it away. He claims he still thought we could win her over, but I don't believe him. I think he secretly agrees with her. She went storming up to the attic, but by the time she got there, Erri was gone. I kept thinking she'd find him hiding behind some of the junk, then I noticed the open window. I thought — I thought —" She broke off and bit her lip. Her face went very red. I thought she was going to cry, so I looked away tactfully.

"What's your mother going to do?" I asked Robert anxiously. "Is she going to tell the police? Does she know Erri's here?"

I had a vision of police cars screaming down our street, stopping at our door, with all the neighbors peering from behind their curtains. Not that I cared for the neighbors, but Auntie Amy would. I imagined the policemen stamping into the hall, disturbing her tea party, and disgracing her in the eyes of her friends. I could almost hear the whispers:

"Do you know what her niece was doing? Hiding an illegal boy in her room. I always thought there was something odd about that girl. The way she creeps about and pretends not to see you . . ."

"Don't look so worried," Robert said. "She doesn't know anything. We've got her completely confused. We told her that it wasn't true, that we'd made it all up. We said we'd done it for a bet."

I thought of the bitterness in Victoria's voice when she'd shouted at her mother. I thought of the fury of the row I'd overheard. "Don't tell me she believed that."

"She wanted to believe it; that's half the battle. We'd shaken her, accused her of being a hypocrite. She realized that was what everyone might think. Poor Mum," Robert said, sounding amused at his mother's predicament.

I glanced at Victoria's face. She didn't look amused at all. Her face was stiff with anger and bitterness. "I used to believe in her," she'd said. I felt sorry for Call-me-Kate. She'd come down from her pedestal with a shattering bump. Not all the king's horses or all the king's men could put her together again in her daughter's eyes. Like Humpty Dumpty, she was a scrambled egg.

"I thought Chris would give us away," Victoria said. Her tears had drained away from her hot eyes. "I'd have killed him if he had. Robert told Mum we'd been talking about the illegal immigrants at Heathrow and I'd said I wished we could have smuggled one home, because Mum would have helped hide him, and Chris had bet me ten pounds she wouldn't, because it would be illegal and she wouldn't do anything illegal. I was watching Chris all the time Robert was talking. I tried to will him to keep his mouth shut, but then Mum turned to him and said, 'Is this true, Christopher?' I could've died."

"What did he say?"

"He stood by us. He said, 'Of course, Mum. That's why Vicky's so mad with you. You made her lose ten pounds. Not that she'll ever pay me. She never has any money.' Chris is a very clever liar," Robert said admiringly. "You wouldn't think so, would you? I mean, he looks so prim and virtuous. I suppose that's why people believe him."

"And of course he's Mum's favorite, that helps," Victoria said.

Robert was watching me. "I don't think we've convinced Lesley," he said. "She still looks worried."

"Supposing she sees him? I can't keep him shut up all the time. Supposing she sees him looking out of a window, like I did?"

"We'll tell her she's imagined it. We'll tell her she's suffering from delusions, just as we told you," Victoria said. "You believed us."

"I didn't! I told you I didn't! I knew he was real."

"Did you?" she asked. "I don't think so. I don't think you're certain even now. There's nobody in there, you know." Her eyes were very bright. She made me feel like a rabbit caught in the headlights of a car. "The room's empty," she said. "It's all in your mind. Erri doesn't exist —"

Suddenly his door opened and he stood there, clutching my sketchbook in his hand, looking like someone uncertain of his welcome.

"Erri!" I cried with such relief that an answering smile lit up his face. "Come in. Have you finished your drawing? Let's see."

Holding out my hands to him, I glanced sideways at Victoria and she laughed. "A few more minutes and I'd have had you standing on your head," she said.

I didn't answer. I was looking at Erri's drawing. It was a picture of war. Three planes flew in a lurid blue sky, dropping bombs on an exploding earth. On the left something burned, scarlet and orange and yellow, a house perhaps, or a tank, it was difficult to tell. Tiny figures ran in all directions, as if not knowing which way to go. In the air above their heads there was a horizontal leg, unattached, drawn completely out of proportion, so that it was bigger than the planes and might have been meant to be an airship, if it hadn't been for the foot, complete with five toes.

It was a picture any boy might have drawn, full of blood and thunder. But the fact that Erri had done it made it terrible. My hand shook.

"What is it?" Victoria snatched the drawing from me and stared at it. I think it shook her too, but she couldn't resist saying, "I told you so. I said there must be war in his country." She turned to him and pointed at the drawing. "This is where you came from, isn't it, Erri?" she asked. "This is your country, your home?"

He spread his hands nervously.

"I'm sure he understands," she muttered, exasperated. "Were you there?" She pointed to one of the tiny running figures. "Is this you? Is this Erri?"

"No!" he cried urgently. "Not Erri! Not Erri." He turned to me and added pleadingly, "Erri here."

I put my arms round his thin shoulders. "Of course you can stay here, Erri. Of course you can."

He smiled.

I looked up and saw Victoria's bitter face. "Easy promises," she said. "Easy promises and tears in your eyes, just like Mum. And how do you think you're going to manage? You can't just let him loose in London, you know, when you're tired of him. Not a kid of his age. You must've heard what can happen to stray kids. So what are you going to do? I bet you haven't got one sensible idea in your head."

"Yes, I have!" I cried rashly. It wasn't true, of course. I had ideas, I always had ideas, but not sensible ones.

"Tell us, then," Victoria said.

The horrid little silence following her words might have grown and given me away, but luck was on my side. We'd never have heard Auntie Amy's light footsteps on the stairs if we'd been talking.

"My aunt's coming!" I whispered, and Erri dived under my bed.

10

She did not come into the room, but smiled at us from the doorway, quite unaware of Erri under the bed.

"I wondered if Victoria and Robert would like to stay to supper," she said. "There's plenty . . ."

I knew she'd bought two pork chops for our meal, and I wasn't surprised to see her look relieved when they refused, saying their mother was expecting them back.

"Another time, perhaps," she said.

"Thank you. We'd like that," Robert said politely.

Victoria said nothing but sat and stared at her with fierce brown eyes. I think she was trying to hypnotize her, to make her go away, because she looked pleased with herself when my aunt retreated downstairs. I could have told her that Auntie Amy was shy with young people, unless they were made of china like the children on the mantelpiece.

"You can come out now, Erri. She's gone," Robert said. "And we'd better go, too. It's nearly suppertime. We don't want Mum coming to fetch us."

I was suddenly frightened. I didn't want them to go and leave Erri behind. I didn't see how I could manage on my own.

"What shall I do with him this evening? I usually watch television with Auntie Amy. Suppose he starts wandering above our heads and she hears him?"

"Lock him in and tell him to be quiet."

"But he can't understand —"

"Put your finger to your lips. He knows what that means."

"What about his food?"

"Sneak it up to his room when your aunt's watching TV," Victoria said impatiently.

I explained about there being only two pork chops.

"What would she have given us?"

"I suppose she'd have opened some cans."

"Give him a can of something, then. Baked beans, anything, he won't mind. As long as there's enough to eat, he'll be happy."

They didn't understand the way we lived. Their chaotic kitchen was probably bulging with food — cake and cold chicken and ham and rice pudding and yesterday's stew and great chunks of different

74

cheeses, all muddled together, some fresh, some already going moldy. I doubted if Call-me-Kate ever planned a meal when her husband was away. "Look in that can and see if we have some cake, Victoria," she'd say, or "I could have sworn there was some cold chicken left. Never mind. Let's have an omelet."

Auntie Amy's cupboards were so tidy that a stolen can would be like a missing front tooth.

"She'd be bound to notice," I said.

"You mean she counts the peas you eat?"

"No. You don't understand. She'd be glad if I ate more, she thinks I'm too thin. But if cans suddenly started vanishing out of her cupboards, she'd be puzzled . . ."

"Can't have that," Robert said. "Mustn't puzzle Aunt Amy. Might give her the wrong idea."

It was easy for him to laugh. He didn't have to worry anymore. Erri was my responsibility now. They could go home and have their supper and not listen for noises above their heads to give them away . . .

"What shall I do?" I asked helplessly.

"Give him half of your pork chop," Victoria told me. "Slip it into a small plastic bag and put it into your pocket when she's not looking."

"I haven't got any small plastic bags."

"You're useless," she said, staring at me with

disgust. "Why did it have to be you? This isn't going to work, Robbie," she added, turning to her brother.

I hated her. She made me feel small and stupid. I wanted to tell her exactly what I thought of her, but I was afraid of bursting into tears. Since my illness, I cry very easily, especially when I'm tired. I was tired now. I wanted to go to bed and pull the covers over my head and never see any of them again.

Erri put his hand on my arm. His small face was strained. I thought perhaps he sensed my anger and it made him afraid. But I was wrong.

"Potty?" he said.

"He wants to go to the bathroom," Victoria explained, as if I weren't capable of working this out for myself.

"I'll take him," I said quickly, and held my hand out to him. "Come on, Erri."

He put his hand into mine trustingly. Without looking at Victoria or Robert, I led him on to the landing and along to the bathroom. "Loo," I said, pointing.

"Loo," he repeated, nodding.

I waited outside.

The door to my room opened and Victoria came out. She glanced at me but didn't say anything. I watched with astonishment as she went quietly into the empty bedroom next to mine, came out again a minute later, and then went into the next one.

How cheeky! Nobody had given her the right to make herself so at home in my aunt's house. What did she think she was doing?

She came out again holding a large china vase with gilt handles and a curly gilt edge and fat pink cherubs holding garlands of red roses on the sides. She smiled at me triumphantly and mouthed something I couldn't understand and carried it off into my room.

I should have guessed, of course.

She'd put it on the floor by his bed. "I didn't think you'd have a potty," she said when we came back and saw it there. "I mean, you don't seem to have anything useful. How do you expect him to manage when you have to lock him in his room? This will do until you find something better."

"No! He can't use that! It belongs to Auntie Amy. It's valuable, an antique —"

"It's hideous," she said.

"It's beautiful! And it's her favorite —"

"If it was, she'd have it downstairs on her mantelpiece," Victoria said reasonably, "instead of those sickly china children."

"They're not sickly. And they're even more valuable," I told her. I tried to remember the names Auntie Amy had told me, the names of the factories.

"They're old, Staffordshire, and — and one of them's Derby!"

She was unimpressed. "All this fuss over a stupid old vase. Just for one night," she muttered.

"Oh, all right," I said, giving in. To be honest, I didn't like the vase either.

Victoria came back after supper, carrying a small nylon totebag. She brushed away Auntie Amy's offers of tea or hot chocolate with a shake of the head. "Full up. Can't stay long," she said. "I've brought the books I promised I'd lend Lesley. I'll just take them up to her room. Come on, Lesley."

"That's kind of you, my dear," Auntie Amy said. I could see she found Victoria an odd sort of girl. Too brusque. Too self-assured. But she was determined to like her for my sake. "Very kind, isn't it, Lesley?"

"Wonderful," I said, and she glanced at me sharply. I had to be careful. My aunt is so soft and vague, it's easy to think she must also be a bit dim, but she isn't, not really. She'd heard the sarcasm in my voice.

I followed Victoria upstairs. She put the totebag on the floor, glanced at the closed door to Erri's room, and sat down on my armchair.

"Robert said I've been horrid to you," she announced.

I shrugged.

"He told me to come and apologize."

I waited.

After a moment, she said crossly, "Oh, all right. I'm sorry. That do?"

"Yes, okay. What's in the totebag?"

"Have a look."

I knelt down on the floor and unzipped it. There was a can of baked beans. Packets of cookies, cheese wrapped up in tinfoil, a whole loaf of brown bread, a can opener and an old bread knife, a pale blue potty in a plastic bag, a box of Legos, and two jigsaws . . .

"And three books for you," she said, "in case she asks to see what I brought."

"Thanks."

We were silent for a moment, neither of us knowing what to say. Then she glanced at the closed door and asked, "Is he asleep?"

"I don't know. Shall I go and see?"

"Yes, but don't wake him."

I turned the handle slowly and pushed the door half open, so that the light from my room would not fall on his bed. He was lying curled up like a stray cat trying to take up as little space as possible so that it wouldn't be noticed and turned out. His eyes were shut, and he looked very young. I found myself wishing he were my brother. I'd always wanted one.

"Poor little squirt," Victoria whispered. "I hope we can keep him safe."

I liked her then.

"You must lock him in," she said after I'd shut the door again.

"He hates it."

"I guess he does, but he's used to it. You can't risk his deciding to explore the house in the middle of the night. Supposing your aunt runs into him in the dark? She's old. She could have a heart attack."

I turned the key.

"That's better," Victoria said. She peered into my face. "Don't look upset. You've got to be tough. You can't help him if you go all soppy and sentimental. You want to help him, don't you?"

"Yes, of course."

She hesitated, still looking at me.

"What's the matter?" I asked.

"Christopher's coming to see you tomorrow," she said. "We think he wants to change your mind for you, about Erri. Don't let him, whatever he says. Don't even listen to him. Shut your ears and think of something else when he's talking." She put her hands on my shoulders and her face so close to mine that our noses nearly touched. "Please, Lesley! Don't let him talk you out of it. Please try to be strong."

I didn't write to my mother that night. I didn't tell her about Erri. It would only worry her and, by the time my letter reached her, it would be out of date. Besides, I knew what she'd say. She'd say I ought to tell my aunt, but I couldn't, not now. I was committed. Oddly enough, it made it easier. There was no point in worrying about it. I went straight to sleep and did not dream of anything.

It was dark when I woke. Someone was screaming, screaming in the night. The noise seemed to be all round me, and for a moment, confused, I wondered if it was I who was screaming. But it was Erri, of course.

11

The light in his room wouldn't work. The bulb must have gone out. I went over to his bed in the dark, saying his name softly, "Erri! Erri!"

He must have been sitting up. My outstretched hands touched first a thin shoulder, then his hair. He was shouting now, his voice hoarse, the words unrecognizable. I pressed his face against my shoulder to muffle his noise. He promptly bit my arm.

I yelped and held him away from me. "Erri, it's me, Lesley. You've had a bad dream, that's all. Ssh! You'll wake my aunt. No noise. Do you understand?"

He must have, for he stopped shouting immediately. I could feel the bed shaking and hear his sobbing breath catch in his throat. I put my arms round him and said quickly, "It's all right. You're safe now. I won't let anything hurt you. Just be quiet."

All the time, I was listening. I could hear nothing except my own whispering voice. Nobody calling out. No footsteps running up the stairs. My aunt's room was at the back, overlooking the garden, and Erri's at the front, with three closed doors and a flight of stairs between them. Still, I felt uneasy.

I tucked the blanket round Erri and put my finger on his lips. "Hush. Don't make a noise. I'll be back in a minute."

Out on the landing, I hung over the banister and stared down into the darkness. All was silent. I could see nothing. I tiptoed to the head of the stairs, and suddenly, out of the shadows on the landing below, a pale figure appeared and began climbing up toward me on noiseless feet. I caught my breath, and the figure stopped dead. For a moment we confronted each other, like two frightened ghosts in the night, then my aunt said, "Lesley, is that you?"

"Yes." I found the light switch and turned it on. I saw my aunt on the stairs, looking up at me. She was wrapped in a glimmering silk dressing gown, dripping with cream lace at neck and wrist. Her faded silvery hair hung in two plaits over her shoulders. She looked grand and a little strange, not at all like her ordinary daytime self. I wondered if her finery had originally been intended for a younger and happier woman, a bride perhaps, whose wedding had been canceled at the last moment.

"The cats woke me up," I told her. "Did you hear them yowling?"

"Cats," she said. "Only cats, then. I'm glad. I thought you were having a nightmare. Was that you shouting?"

"Yes, I'm sorry. I was trying to frighten the cats away. I didn't mean to wake you."

"I was already up," she told me. "Otherwise I don't suppose I'd have heard anything. It's so hot tonight, isn't it? I was going down to the kitchen to make myself some tea. Would you like anything? Some milk? Some lemonade?"

"No, thanks. I think I'll go back to bed. I'm sleepy."

"Shall I come and tuck you in?" she asked.

"You can't tuck in a comforter," I told her. "Good night, Auntie Amy."

"Good night, my dear."

She turned and went down the stairs without looking back. Was she suspicious? I didn't think so. It's true she'd never come up before to tuck me in, but then we'd never met in the middle of the night like this. There was something friendly about it, two people awake in a sleeping world. I would have liked to go down to the kitchen with her and

84

have milk and cookies and talk. I felt we would have gotten to know each other better. But of course there was a third person awake. I had to go back to Erri.

It was just as well I did. When I switched on my light, I found him sitting in my armchair with his blanket round his shoulders.

"Erri!"

"Not sleep," he said.

"You must. Go back to your room. Auntie Amy's up and about. Supposing she'd come in here and found you? You've got to hide."

"Hide," he repeated, clutching a word he obviously knew. He looked at the space under my bed.

"Not there. In your room. In your own bed. I'll lock the door and you'll be safe."

But he was reluctant to go back into the dark little room. When I tried to push him through the door, he clung to me, though he did not make any noise. I think he was frightened that his nightmare was waiting for him there. I knew that feeling. Often, waking from a bad dream, I would sit bolt upright with my eyes wide open, determined not to sleep again until morning.

I should have insisted. Victoria would have, and she would have been right. I took a terrible risk. I left my bedside light on and let him stay in my room, sitting on the floor on the far side of my bed, so that he could duck underneath if we heard Auntie Amy coming. Not that she makes much noise; she walks as quietly as I do, and, knowing the house so well, often doesn't bother to switch on the lights, passing through the dim passages like a familiar ghost. But she always knocks on my door before coming in.

We sat for what seemed like hours, listening to the old house creaking around us and the wind whispering in the garden. Three times Erri dived under the bed, but only for false alarms. Nobody knocked at the door. To pass the time, I taught him to play ticktacktoe, silently. He soon picked it up. When he won, he put his hand over his mouth, as if to prevent a cry of triumph escaping. I remembered Robert saying, "Don't worry. He's very quick and quiet. He won't give you away." It was true. Erri was like none of the small boys I knew. He reminded me of a dog I'd once seen, a cowed-looking creature crouching in the long grass at the edge of a field, its eyes watching us anxiously as we approached. It did not move until we were almost level with it; then it sprang to its feet and backed away, its tail wagging feebly but its lips curling to show its teeth, in a contradictory way.

"Don't touch it, Lesley," my mother had warned me. "It looks as if it's been ill-treated, poor beast. It might bite."

Erri had bitten me, I remembered, and looked down at my arm. He had not bitten hard. There were toothmarks visible, but the skin was only bruised, not broken. Erri, who saw where I was looking, whispered anxiously, "Hurt?"

"No." If Auntie Amy had noticed, surely she would have said something. She hadn't been wearing her glasses . . . "It's all right," I said.

Erri began talking in his own language, but I hushed him. We went on playing ticktacktoe until the sky lightened and our eyelids grew heavy. Then I took him into his room and tucked him into bed and sat beside him. I thought he'd never go to sleep. It was ten past four before I got back to my room. I wanted to stay awake so that I could plan what to say to Christopher when he came, but I feel asleep immediately.

The young Harwoods came in the early afternoon. They must have been waiting for my aunt to leave the house, because the bell rang only a minute or two after she'd gone, and there they were on the doorstep, all three of them in a bunch.

"How long is she going to be out?" Victoria asked.

"She said she wouldn't be long. She's only gone to the corner shop."

"You'd better get ready quickly. We're going to the park. We can talk there," Christopher said. His eyes were blue like his mother's, but colder. He was very good-looking. My friends would've raved about him, but he made me nervous. "Leave a note for your aunt saying you've come out for a walk with us, and tell her you'll be back for supper. That should give us plenty of time. Right?"

"What about Erri?"

"We're taking him with us," Robert told me. "We've brought him some shoes, and a soccer ball of Robert's to play with. He'll be all right. We can smuggle him out the back way, so that we don't risk meeting your aunt. It won't matter if we're seen with him in the park. We could say he just attached himself to us. It'll do him good to have some fresh air, poor little beast."

"Supposing he runs away?"

"He won't," Christopher said, adding half under his breath, "No such luck."

Victoria turned on him angrily, and he told her he was only joking. Nobody believed him.

Erri, when we fetched him, did not want to leave the house. Perhaps he thought we were going to hand him over to the police. "No," he kept saying. "No. Not go." We all told him we were only going to the park. Park, we said. Place with trees

88

and flowers, where you could play games and run about.

He still looked worried. Perhaps he didn't trust us. "Erri, I swear I'll never —" I began, but Christopher must have guessed from the expression on my face the sort of thing I meant to say, because he took hold of my arm, pulling me back.

"Don't commit yourself. Don't make promises you can't keep," he said in a low voice. "Wait till we've discussed it."

I remembered how young and powerless I was. And I kept silent, leaving Victoria to persuade Erri to come out with us.

12

It was very hot in the park. Old men dozed on the benches, their fat elderly dogs sleeping in their shadows. Small children crouched over their castles in the sandbox, while their mothers yawned and gossiped in the sun. There were not many people of our age. The park was small, and there was nothing much to do there except lie in the sun or try to tempt the overfed ducks on the pond with crusts of bread. Notices told us to KEEP OFF THE GRASS.

"There's nowhere for him to play," Victoria said.

"Yes, there is," Robert told her. "Follow me."

He led us past the duck pond, down a narrow, curving path between high evergreens, until we came to a large area of yellowing grass, on which three boys were playing with a soccer ball. They can't have been older than I was, but they looked huge compared to Erri, big and tough and unfriendly. They scowled when they caught sight of the ball he was carrying. They were here first. They didn't want small kids getting under their feet.

"You can't expect him to play with them," Victoria said. "They'd murder him."

"Not while I'm around," Robert said. "Anyway, who said he was going to play with them? He's going to play with me. Come on, Erri!"

I didn't want Robert to go. He was the only one of the Harwoods whom I liked. I'd counted on his support.

"I'll come too!" I cried and tried to follow, but Christopher and Victoria held me back, one on either side. I felt like a bone between two dogs.

"We were going to talk, remember?" Christopher said. "Let's sit in the shade over there. The grass is quite dry. Would you like my jacket to sit on?"

"Now isn't that kind of him?" Victoria jeered. "Beware, Lesley. Chris is only kind when he wants to get something from you —"

"Be quiet, Vicky!" her brother said. "You agreed you'd let me have my say without interrupting. You'll have your turn later. Why don't you join Robert and Erri? I'll call you when I've finished."

"I want to hear what you say. I'll keep my mouth shut," she promised.

"No heavy sighs or head shaking?"

"No. Only she mustn't decide anything till I've had my turn."

"All right," he agreed.

He turned his back on her. Then he leaned toward me, put his face very near mine, and began talking gently in a soft, sensible sort of voice, smiling kindly. He told me that every country had to have some immigration laws, we couldn't let everyone in, especially not a small country like Britain. We didn't have enough jobs or houses for everyone as it was. "Think of the people sleeping in cardboard boxes in winter," he said. "Think of old ladies dying of hypothermia. Think of the unemployed."

I tried to think of them, but I was distracted by the closeness of his face. I could see the pores in his nose and the tiny red veins in the whites of his eyes. The stubble on his chin was uneven, as if he'd trimmed it with blunt scissors.

"I feel just as sorry for Erri as you do," he said, sighing into my face. "But it won't work, it just won't work. I've thought and thought about it. I've agonized about it." He ran his hands through his hair till it stood up in two wings like a disturbed angel's. "I simply can't see any way out. You'll have to tell your aunt. Or better still, I'll tell my mother. You needn't come into it at all — shut up, Vicky.

You said I could have my turn," he shouted when she tried to interrupt. He turned back to me. "Just think seriously for a moment. You can't keep him cooped up in a small room forever. How long are you planning to hide him? A week? A year? Ten years? You'll be lucky if you can manage another day or two without your aunt finding out. She's not deaf, is she? Or blind?"

I thought of last night. He was right. I could not keep Erri. It had been a mad idea. Better let him tell his mother, who would know whom to get in touch with, how to get a lawyer for Erri . . .

"You see how impossible it is," Christopher said gently. "He'd be far happier in a refugee camp with his own people."

"No!" Victoria burst out. "They'd send him back and he'd be killed! Don't you remember those banners the people were carrying? 'To send them back is murder!' That's what they said!"

"They wouldn't send him back if he was in any danger, not a child, not anyone," Christopher told her. "Dad says they go into each case very carefully —"

"Those protesters didn't think so. Nor did Mum! She said governments make mistakes just like anyone else, only they make bigger ones. She said we oughtn't to turn *anyone* away. They were always quarreling about it, you know they were. Dad got really angry, but she stood her ground. She said it was inhuman to send people back —" Victoria broke off. Her hot brown eyes filled with tears, and she turned her head away to hide them. "She did say so. I heard her. I believed her. Why, Chris? Why should she pretend? I can't understand —"

He said gently, "I suppose she changed her mind. People do. Don't let it upset you, Vicky. After all," he added, spoiling his kindness, "Dad is okay about it."

They started arguing again. My head began to spin. The more carefully I tried to listen, the more confused I got. When Christopher was speaking, I believed him. Then, when I listened to Victoria, I believed her.

It was very hot. I looked across the grass. Robert and Erri had been throwing the ball to each other, but now they stopped. Robert took off his T-shirt, threw it down, and held out his hand to Erri, saying something I couldn't hear. Erri shook his head and backed away, clutching his T-shirt as if frightened that Robert would try and snatch it from him. Robert shrugged. Erri then slipped off his shoes and handed them to Robert, who walked off and dropped them on the grass a little distance away. I'd watched boys playing soccer in the park at home. I knew a makeshift goal when I saw one. It wasn't that that puzzled me.

Victoria must have noticed that I was no longer listening to them. She looked over to see what had caught my attention.

"What is it?" she asked.

"I was wondering why Erri didn't want to take off his shirt."

"Shall I tell you why? Shall I?" she demanded. "It's because his back is covered with scars from where he's been beaten. But Christopher doesn't care! He wants to get rid of him, even if it means sending him back to his death!"

Christopher flushed so dark that his pale blue eyes looked like chinks of light in a crimson mask. His voice, rising in anger, lost years and became as shrill as a small boy's complaining of injustice —

"That's not fair!"

The words rang out loudly, and everyone in sight turned round to stare at him: Robert and Erri, the three soccer-playing boys, and a fat woman with a tiny white scrap of a dog. This little creature, excited by the noise, ran over and started yelping round Christopher's ankles and snapping at his trousers with teeth like pins.

Christopher looked so angry, I was afraid he would kick the dog, but instead he picked it up and, holding it at arm's length, presented it to its owner, saying with icy dignity, "I think this is yours, madam."

"That's no way to hold an animal," the woman said aggressively, snatching it from him and cradling it in her arms. "You should support the back legs, like this. Poor little fellow, was the nasty boy unkind to you?"

"Was your nasty dog unkind to my brother, that's more to the point," Victoria cried, instantly forgetting her quarrel with Christopher. "Look, it's torn his trousers! There's probably blood underneath . . . Dangerous dogs should wear muzzles. There's a law that says so."

The three boys who'd left their soccer game to listen now joined in.

"That a pit bull terrier you got there, missus?" asked one, grinning.

"Nah, it's a rottweiler," another said, and they all sniggered.

Robert, coming over, looked concerned. "Has it really bitten you, Chris? You've got to be careful with dog bites. You could get tetanus."

"It's nothing," Christopher said irritably.

I thought he ought to be grateful. I wished I had a brother and sister who'd break off in the middle of a quarrel to rush to my support, closing ranks against any outsider foolish enough to attack. I felt almost sorry for the woman, with her red face and her tiny white dog. She was now backing away, mumbling, "He's only a puppy. He only wanted to play . . ."

They'd forgotten Erri. He was alone. He didn't have anyone to rush to his support. Only me, and what good was I? I didn't have anyone either. No good counting on Auntie Amy. She was kind, but she was old. Old people are cautious. She'd agree with their dad and Christopher that the government knew best. She wouldn't keep Erri, not against the law. She'd cry, but she'd hand him over. Then she'd go back to dusting her china children, holding them carefully, lovingly in her hands.

13

Christopher was sulking. He strode along ahead of us, stiff-necked, stiff-legged, like a dog wondering whether to fight.

We trailed behind him. We were going to the café in the middle of the park. Nothing had been decided. We were all hot and sticky. Erri was holding my hand, and Victoria and Robert were both trying to get on the other side of me, pushing and shoving.

"It's my turn to talk to her!" Victoria said.

"If it's anyone's, it's mine," Robert retorted. "I heard you and Chris shouting at her. You'd rather talk to me, wouldn't you, Lesley?"

"I want to talk to Christopher," I said. "Alone."

"What!"

They stared at me in disgust, as if I were a traitor. Even Erri's eyes accused me, as if he'd understood what I'd said. He'd heard Christopher's name, of course. He must've sensed that Christopher wanted to be rid of him.

"He's getting cross," I explained, "with all of us against him. I thought if I spoke to him alone, it might calm him down."

"He'll talk you round," Victoria said. "He's very persuasive."

"He won't persuade me. I'm not as feeble as you think."

They stared at me doubtfully. Then Robert said, "Let her try. She's got a point. It's no good going on at him. Never has been. But she might get round him. Try fluttering your eyelashes," he advised me.

"Don't be an idiot! She's only a kid. And not pretty enough for that sort of thing, anyway," Victoria told him.

"Don't you think so?"

They both looked at me consideringly, and I could feel myself blushing.

"What are you planning to say to him?" Victoria demanded.

"That he can leave it to me. That I know what I'm doing —"

"He'll never believe that!" they said immediately. But they agreed to give me a chance.

*   *   *

99

We sat at separate tables in the small café; Robert and Victoria with Erri by the window, and Christopher with me on the far side. I was horribly embarrassed and let the silence grow too long.

"Well?" he said. "I thought you wanted to talk to me. Here I am."

His voice, his face, his eyes, all were so cold, he might have been made of ice. When he sipped his hot coffee, I half expected him to begin to melt onto the table and drip onto the floor. I wished he would. Then the woman behind the counter would come and mop him up and pour him down the drain, and I'd have nothing to worry about.

"Well?" he said again, raising his eyebrows.

"I know you're clever," I began. "Everyone says so."

"Have you got something in your eye?" he demanded, staring at me.

I flushed and shook my head. So much for Robert's advice.

"So everyone says I'm clever, do they?" he said. "Who is everyone? Not Victoria, I think. Nor Robert. And your aunt hardly knows me."

"No, but she's heard a lot about you!" I cried rashly.

"Really? You intrigue me. Who from?"

"People. Neighbors. Your mother."

"My mother," he said, and laughed. "Very well. Let's accept the fact that I'm very clever. Does that mean you're going to accept my advice?"

"Well, not exactly . . . I mean, I can see you're right. It wouldn't work for you. But it's different for me. It wouldn't matter so much if I got found out. I'm young and I've been ill. I wouldn't get into much trouble. I'd cry and they'd be sorry for me. Nobody else would suffer. I'd say I helped him all by myself. I wouldn't bring you into it —"

"I'm not afraid for myself!" he said. Very stiff and offended. I wasn't doing this well.

"I know you're not," I told him quickly. "I know it's your dad you're thinking of. It wouldn't be fair to him to risk his job —"

"For a stupid, childish, sentimental venture that's bound to fail. As I've already explained. Good grief, I thought you were listening to all my arguments. I thought you were agreeing with me. You nodded your head. Twice."

"It was so hot," I said apologetically. "I was sleepy."

He hit the table with his hands so hard that his cup rattled, and the coffee slopped into the saucer. "It's useless talking to you," he said, and pushed back his chair.

I caught hold of his hand in both of mine.

"Please, please let me try. I do so want to help him. Give me a chance! I won't get your dad into trouble. It's nothing to do with your family anymore. If I get found out, I'll say you didn't know anything about it. They won't know he was ever in your attic, how can they? I'll say I found him somewhere. Not Heathrow . . . somewhere else. I know! I'll say he fell off the back of a truck —"

He laughed at that and called me a silly kid. I didn't mind if he found me comic. I could see he was weakening. He didn't give in immediately. He insisted on telling me his arguments all over again. I didn't listen. I was afraid he might convince me. I just looked at him hopefully.

By the time we joined the others at their table, I had his promise not to tell. A qualified promise. He wouldn't tell unless something happened that forced him to change his mind. He wouldn't tell without warning me first what he was going to do. He would expect me to keep my word not to involve his father in any way.

"Of course," I said.

"That means you mustn't ask Robert or Vicky for help. You mustn't drag them into it."

My heart sank. How could I manage without them?

"Do you agree?" he asked, beginning to frown.
"Yes."

He turned to his brother and sister. "And you two, do you agree?"

"Yes, Christopher," they said.

"Good." He smiled with quiet satisfaction, like a lawyer who'd just won his case, and smoothed down his ruffled fair hair with his hands.

But he hadn't won, I thought with secret glee. I had. Then I caught sight of Erri, who was watching us anxiously, and I realized that it wasn't a game we'd been playing. Or, if it was, there would be only one loser if things went wrong, and that was Erri.

That night I put a clean handkerchief in my pocket before going down to supper. We were having spaghetti and meatballs. Unless we had guests, we always ate in the kitchen at the small table by the window. I sat opposite Auntie Amy. Pulling my chair well in, so that she couldn't see what I was doing, I spread the hanky carefully over my lap. Then I pushed a meatball around and wished the telephone would ring or someone would come to the door or run screaming down the road, anything to distract her attention from me. She kept glancing at my plate, but she didn't say anything.

I sniffed. "I can smell gas," I said, untruthfully.

She went over to the stove to check that the

burners had been turned off properly. I quickly scooped three meatballs and a great dollop of tangled spaghetti onto my lap.

"They're all turned off," she said, coming back. "Are you sure you smelled gas? I can't smell anything."

I sniffed again and shook my head. "I can't smell it now."

"I hope there's not a leak."

"I guess I imagined it."

She still looked worried. "They say you don't notice it after a while," she said. "I wonder if I ought to ring the Gas Board."

"No! It might not've been gas at all I smelled. Perhaps it was the meatballs." I bent down and sniffed the solitary meatball left on my plate. "Yes, it was. Sorry."

"They're not as bad as all that," she said, smiling. Her eyes went to my plate. Then she looked up at me again thoughtfully. I could feel the sauce seeping through the hanky on my lap and through my denim trousers, warm and clammy and horrible on my bare skin.

She said gently, "Lesley, if there's any food you simply hate, you've only to say so, my dear. I always hated lamb fat as a child. It made me feel sick. At school we were told to finish everything on our plates. I remember hiding revolting lumps of con-

gealing fat in my hanky, even in my pockets —"
She broke off, seeing me blush, and laughed. "Is
that what you've done? I thought I'd never seen
three meatballs disappear so quickly. Never mind,
love. Come on, give me your plate — and your
hanky or whatever you've put it in — and I'll
throw the nasty stuff away. What would you like
instead? Fish sticks? Scrambled eggs?"

She was so kind, but as I scraped the spaghetti
and meatballs from my hanky into the wastebasket,
I wished she'd leave me alone, go away, disappear.
Poor Erri would go supperless tonight.

I had failed twice. No supper for Erri, and no
bed. Auntie Amy had been in the kitchen ever
since we returned from the park. I hadn't had a
chance to smuggle him into the house and up the
stairs. He was sitting on a sack of peat in the cob-
webby gloom of our small garden shed. I had
turned the key on him, frightened he would get
bored with waiting for me to come, and make off
toward the bright, dangerous lights of the city. Now,
as I sat eating my fish sticks under my aunt's eye, I
worried in case he might panic in the dark and
start hammering at the shed door and screaming.

I needn't have worried. When at last I got a
chance to slip out into the garden, leaving my aunt
dozing in front of the television, I found that
Robert and Victoria were with him. They were

eating cheese sandwiches and cake. As soon as Christopher had gone out with his friends, they had come round. Neither of them, it appeared, had any intention of leaving Erri to me.

"You'd be bound to make a mess of it without us," Victoria said. "Just look what you did. You locked Erri in here but forgot to remove the key. If Erri had been clever, he could have turned it from the inside with — oh, I don't know — two bits of wire or something. Or your aunt might have decided she needed her clippers and found him. You're just like Robert, you never think. Erri told us you haven't even given him any supper yet. It's a good thing we brought sandwiches."

Robert winked at me, and I smiled. I was getting used to Victoria.

"What about your promise to Christopher?" I asked.

"What promise?" they said. "We didn't promise anything. All we agreed was that *you* mustn't ask us for help. Well, you haven't, have you? We're volunteers."

14

"You look tired, Lesley," my aunt said the next morning at breakfast. "Didn't you sleep well?"

"It was so hot," I said.

It hadn't been the heat that had kept me awake. It had been Erri. He'd had another bad dream, though he hadn't screamed this time, merely whimpered in his sleep. I'd been awake, sitting in my chair by the open window, working on a plan; otherwise I wouldn't have heard him.

I went to him and stroked his hair back from his forehead. His skin was moist with sweat. It was like an oven in his small, airless room. I'd have to get his window to open tomorrow . . . I sat beside him for some time. Then I went back to bed, leaving the door open between our rooms. At six o'clock my alarm woke me.

"You must get up long before your aunt does," Victoria had told me the night before, "so that you

107

can smuggle Erri out of the house before she wakes and hide him behind the shed. Or in it, if it rains. Tell your aunt tonight that you'll be spending the day with me tomorrow, in case she thinks of something else for you to do. I'll come by for you at ten."

"Why don't you go back to bed for an hour or two?" my aunt suggested now. "I could ring Victoria —"

"No, I'm fine, honest," I said quickly.

We went to the park again, and sat on the grass watching Erri play with the three soccer-playing boys. Recognizing him from yesterday, they had greeted him like an old friend and asked him to join them.

"He doesn't understand much English," I'd told them. "He comes from abroad."

"That doesn't matter," one of them said. "I don't understand it either, and I come from jest round the corner."

They put him in the goal, which seemed unfair as he was so much smaller than they were and did not stand a chance. Not that he seemed to mind. He leaped about quite happily, missing every ball.

"We have to make plans," Victoria said. "We can't just drift . . . Lesley, are you listening?"

"Yes."

I already had a plan. I hadn't told Victoria about it yet, because I'd wanted to try it out on Robert first, but he was not here today. He and Christopher had gone out with their mother for the day to visit some old friends in the country. Victoria had refused to go with them, saying she'd rather stay at home.

"Mum didn't dare try and make me go," she'd said, with a kind of bitter satisfaction. "She knows I despise her. She keeps trying to get round me. Look!" She brought a ten-pound bill out of her pocket and showed it to me. "She gave me this and told me to treat you to lunch. Blood money."

I was shocked by the way she spoke of her mother, but I didn't say anything, not wanting her to turn her anger on me. She was such a fierce girl. I was half afraid of her.

We watched Erri in silence for a minute, then she said, "Robert and I have been talking things over. He thinks we ought to telephone Erri's embassy and find out if they can help. Without giving names, of course. Just a general inquiry."

"Which embassy? We don't know what country he comes from," I pointed out, smiling.

"Oh, I'll soon get it out of him," she told me with her usual confidence.

"Want to bet?"

"All right. Fifty cents, if you're sure you can afford to lose it. Erri!" she shouted. "Come over here! We want you."

He muttered something to the boys, then ran over and flung himself down on the grass beside us.

She waited till the other boys had started playing again, then leaned forward and said, "Erri, you must tell us now what country you come from, so that we can help you, understand?" He hesitated, and she went on softly, "I am your friend, you know that. Who helped you escape? Me. Who hid you in her anorak? Me. Who brings you food every day? Me. You can trust me. Tell me, Erri, what country do you come from? You" — she tapped him on the chest —"where from?"

He glanced at me and then quickly away again. "I can't re-mem-ber," he said carefully. "I had bad acc-i-dent. I can't re-mem-ber this."

I had trained him well, but he was no actor. A parrot would have sounded more convincing.

Victoria stared at him. Then she looked at me. "I suppose this is your doing. How long did it take you to teach him to say that? And what's the idea?"

"They can't send him back if they don't know where he comes from," I said.

"So that's your great plan." She thought about it for a minute, then said regretfully, "Good try, but it wouldn't work. They'd guess he must be one of those missing from that group at Heathrow."

"Not necessarily. The longer we can keep him hidden, the better. There'll be other refugees coming in. He could be from anywhere. It'll confuse them."

"They'll be able to tell by his language —"

"Erri, say something in your own language," I instructed him.

"I can't re-mem-ber. I had bad acc-i-dent. I can't re-mem-ber this," Erri said.

"He sounds like a talking doll. Pull the strings and out the words come. Didn't you teach him anything else? Hey, Erri, tell me, which of us do you like better, me or Lesley?"

"I can't re-mem-ber. I had bad acc-i-dent. I can't re-mem-ber this."

Victoria burst out laughing, and I joined in. Erri looked bewildered, but I thought he was putting it on. He knew the word "like," after all. I think he understood Victoria's last question perfectly well and had avoided answering it very cleverly.

Things were better between Victoria and me after that. I think she was quite taken with my idea, because she went on talking about it, saying that I must try to get Erri to vary the three sentences I'd

111

taught him so he would sound more natural. We agreed that he must never speak a word of his old language again, only English from now on.

"You'd better talk to him as much as you can, just say anything that comes into your mind, it doesn't matter what. That way he'll pick it up," she said. "He understands quite a lot already, more than he lets on."

I looked at Erri, who was tearing the grass with his fingers, apparently intent on making a little pile of it. "He's so quiet."

"I wonder what your aunt would say if she found out about him," Victoria said. "She'd probably have a heart attack. I don't know, though. It's not easy to guess how she'd react. She's a bit of a weirdo, isn't she?"

"What do you mean?" I asked indignantly.

Victoria shrugged. "Well, it's a bit spooky, isn't it? I mean, her being there all alone in that big house, surrounded by rooms full of china babies. Nothing living. Not even a dog or a cat. And then you come, looking like a ghost, creeping around without a sound, peering out of windows . . . I wonder how she'd get on with an ordinary noisy child? Not that you can call him an ordinary child," she said, nodding her head at Erri, who was still absorbed in making little piles of grass. "He's even quieter than you are. Of course, that might appeal to her. Do you think she'd like him?"

"I don't know," I said.

I looked across at him. He was sitting back on his heels. He'd arranged his torn grass in a circle and put two dark stones in the center for eyes and a curved line of daisies for a smiling mouth.

"Who's that meant to be?" I asked.

"Me," he said.

I was going to say it didn't look much like him when he smiled up at me, his teeth as white as the daisies. I wondered if he missed his mother. It had never occurred to me to kiss him good night. Probably it had never occurred to Auntie Amy to kiss me good night either. It didn't mean she didn't like me. I guess she thought I was too old for kisses, just as Robert probably thought I was too young. Erri was only a small kid, however. Perhaps he still needed to be kissed.

"Do you know what Mum said?" Victoria asked. "Mum said she didn't know how your aunt could live in that big house all alone, when there're so many people without homes, sleeping in cardboard boxes, freezing in winter — mind you, Mum's a hypocrite. We've got a spare room that'll take two, and we could fit at least six in the attic if we really tried. But that doesn't occur to her. Oh, no. It's your aunt who ought to move to a one-room flat and give her house to the poor."

"Auntie Amy was born in that house," I said. "Her parents gave it to her when she married, so she's been there all her life. She said once that all her happy memories are there ... She knows it's too big for her, but she can't bear the thought of leaving it. Besides, she works at home. She couldn't possibly manage in a one-room flat — and where would I sleep?"

"All right, calm down. I don't care where she lives," Victoria said. "Let's go to the café and get something to eat. I'll treat you both if you choose something cheap. Otherwise you can pay for yourselves."

That evening, as I was going to the corner shop to buy some chocolate for Erri, I met Mrs. Harwood.

"Hello, Lesley," she said, smiling at me. "You're looking much better. You've got some color in your cheeks."

"I feel better, thank you." I tried to sidle past her, but she put her hand on my shoulder and it seemed rude to jerk away, so I stopped.

"I'm glad you and Victoria are seeing more of each other now," she said. "It's nice for her to have a friend next door."

I wasn't certain what to say to this. While I was trying to decide between "I hope so" or "and for me too," she went on in a rush, "Victoria's a bit cross with me at the moment. There was a silly misunderstanding . . . I don't know if she's told you about it?" She bent down to look right into my eyes, as if she would search out the truth. Her own eyes were miserable. I felt sorry for her, but what could I do? Victoria was my friend now. I had to be on her side.

"No. She hasn't told me anything," I lied.

"I thought she might've." She drew in her breath, sighing. "But I suppose you wouldn't tell me even if she had, would you? No, I can see you couldn't. Don't worry, Lesley. It was just . . . I suppose I hoped to get you to tell her that, well, that I'm sorry. That it was only because she took me by surprise. It's no good my telling her. She won't listen to me. Everyone makes mistakes, especially if someone suddenly springs something on you, so you don't have time to think . . . Can you understand that, Lesley?"

"Yes, Mrs. Harwood."

"Call me Kate," she said, "and put in a good word for me . . . You must have seen the boy. What is he like?"

"What boy?" My heart was hammering.

She looked down at me for a moment, then she

said, "Silly of me, I forgot. Of course, there wasn't any boy. They made him up, didn't they? It was all a joke."

"I don't understand."

"No, of course you don't, my dear," she said, patting my shoulder. Then she strode off down the street on her long legs and left me staring after her.

15

In the garden, the long grass behind the shed was still wet with dew. I saw Erri shiver in the cool morning air. He was so thin. He had no fat to keep out the cold. I must ask Victoria if she could find me a man's raincoat to use as a groundsheet and some warmer clothes than the ones I'd chosen.

"It's not stealing," she'd told me yesterday when she invited me to take what I wanted out of the Save the Children jumble she'd collected. "He's a child and we're saving him, they can't possibly object. Besides, we helpers always have first choice. It's only fair."

I wished Victoria would hurry. My aunt would be getting up soon. Then she would go and have her bath. Fifteen minutes lying in the hot water and listening to the radio, ten minutes to dress and comb her hair, then she'd stand on the landing and call up the stairs, "Lesley! Are you awake? Breakfast in fifteen minutes." And I must be there to answer her, not out in the garden, hiding behind the shed with Erri.

I looked up at the gap between our houses and saw the signals hanging from my window, a green T-shirt and a white towel showing up plainly against the old brick. Erri followed my gaze.

"Green for garden," he said.

"That's right. Clever boy. And what's white for?"

He hesitated, screwing up his face in thought. "Wish you come?"

"Nearly. 'Wish you were here.' And the third signal? The one I haven't hung out?"

"Red for danger," he said promptly.

"Well done."

He smiled proudly.

"Your English is getting much better," I told him. "Victoria said it would if we kept talking to you."

As if in answer to her name, there was a rustling of leaves, and Victoria's head appeared over the wall.

"I could've gone on sleeping for hours," she complained. "Why do we have to get up so early? Can't you train your aunt to keep reasonable hours? It's as bad as being back at school."

She climbed over the wall and dropped down

beside us. "Why did you put out the white as well as the green? Has anything happened?" she asked.

I told her about her mother stopping me, and what she'd said. She scowled.

"Tell me again. What did she say exactly?"

"She said, 'You must have seen the boy. What is he like?' "

"And what did you say?"

"I said, 'What boy?' "

"I bet your face gave you away. I bet you blushed and stammered."

"No, I didn't. Then she said, 'Silly of me. Of course, there wasn't any boy. They made him up.' And I pretended I didn't understand what she meant."

"She'll have guessed," Victoria said gloomily. "She's good at guessing. You don't know her. She's already suspicious. You should see her peering round the house as if she half expects to see illegal immigrants hiding under every chair. She probably wonders why we are suddenly so friendly with you. Perhaps we'd better not see so much of each other."

I must've looked alarmed because she laughed and said, "Don't worry, we won't desert you. We really won't, you know. This is the best thing we've ever done." She looked at Erri. "When I remember how frightened he was — I could hear his teeth chattering, he was shaking so much. And they were going to send him back to — wherever he'd come from. Murder, that's what it would've been, like the sign said. To send them back is murder. *We* saved him. You don't think we'd abandon him now. I'd risk anything, prison or —"

"Would we go to prison?" I asked. "Just for hiding him?"

"Oh, I don't know," she said carelessly. "It might be just reform school or a fine or something like that. It doesn't matter. It'd be worth it, wouldn't it?" She turned to me, her face glowing. "I'm going to be a doctor, if I can pass the exams. I'm not as clever as Christopher, but I think I can do it. Then I'll go out and help people. I won't just stay in England. I want to see all these places. I've always wanted to, ever since I saw my first rain forest poster. D'you know, I used to be afraid that they'd sort out all the trouble in the world before I was old enough to go and help." She laughed. "I needn't have worried, need I? I want to go everywhere, all the beautiful places ... Africa, India, China, Burma, Sri Lanka," she chanted softly, as if there was a magic in the names.

"Can I come with you?" I asked, catching fire from her bright vision.

She looked at me in surprise, then said, "Yes, if

you want to. But you'd have to train to be a doctor or a nurse or something."

Though I admired Victoria and had begun to like her, I was never quite at ease with her. I was secretly glad the next day when she had to go out with her mother and Robert came by himself. He was easy to be with. He made us forget the dangers.

Victoria was strict. She insisted that we only go to the dull little park and to a shabby café in a gray street, where nobody who knew her was ever likely to go. Robert did not worry. He was an optimist. He took us to Whitestone's Pond, where boys and grown men sail their toy boats. We couldn't afford a boat, but Robert had made Erri one out of paper. He wrote the name ERRI on the side, and we set it off among the other boats. It sailed bravely at first, blown by the wind, but then a larger boat knocked it over, and when we last saw it, it was floating on its side, half submerged in the water, with the name washed out. A woman made a disapproving remark about people throwing litter into the water.

Robert was good with his hands. The next day he made us a kite and took us to Parliament Fields to fly it. There were people there with kites shaped like butterflies or birds, bright as summer flowers, scarlet and yellow and purple. Some fluttered just above our heads, some were so high that they speckled the sky. We watched them without envy. We were in a holiday mood.

Robert named his kite after me, writing LESLEY across the top with a red felt pen. When at last, after several unsuccessful attempts, it raced up into the sky, tugging at its string like a dog on a lead, we cheered and clapped our hands. "Go! Go! Go!" we shouted. Nobody made more noise than we did on that windy hilltop. Even Erri, who was usually so quiet and careful when he spoke, shouted with us, though he stopped when he saw me looking at him.

Suddenly the kite dipped down and landed on the grass. Before we could reach it, a dog jumped on it. Its owner called it away, but it was too late. The paper was ripped, the thin struts broken. Half my name was torn off. The man came over and apologized for his dog and offered us money to buy another, but Robert said it didn't matter.

"You should've taken the money," I said when the man had gone.

"I can always make another."

"It won't be the same." I looked at the broken kite in his hands. "You make a boat with Erri's name on it and it sinks. You make a kite with my name on it and it's wrecked. It's a good thing I'm not superstitious."

Robert looked closely at my face. "You are! I can see you are! What can I do to make it right? I know. Just a minute." He looked down and shook his head. "No, I don't fancy the grass. There're too many dogs around."

"What are you looking for?"

"Something edible."

"I've got some chocolate."

I handed it to him. He unwrapped it, broke off two pieces, and, sitting down on the grass, wrote carefully on the chocolate while we watched in bewilderment.

"What are you doing?"

"Writing your names. Erri. Lesley. That's it." He put both pieces in his mouth and ate them.

"What did you do that for?"

"I'm a bad luck–eater," he said. "Like they used to have sin-eaters in the past. I read about it some-where. They used to pay beggars to eat the sins of rich people who died. They'd put food out on the coffin, and the beggars would eat it and get a free meal and a few cents for taking the sins onto them-selves, see?"

I stared at him. "But I don't want you to have bad luck, Robert!"

He hugged me and laughed. "I won't. I don't believe in it. I'm not silly and superstitious."

He was right not to worry. I don't know what went wrong with his bad luck–eating. Perhaps the writing didn't show up clearly enough on the chocolate. It wasn't he who had the bad luck. It was Erri and I.

16

The fine weather broke, that was the first unlucky thing. In the morning, the sky was dark and the rain fell steadily, earnestly, as if to wash the last of the summer away. I listened to it pattering on the flat roof of the Harwoods' garage. It reminded me that it would soon be September. The Harwoods would be going back to their boarding schools and I would start at Redwood Comprehensive. And Erri?

"He'll have to stay in his room and keep quiet while I'm out," I'd said when we'd talked about it the day before.

"All day? He'll be bored out of his mind. And what about the evenings, how can you take him out? Remember, we won't be here. You'll need new friends to help you."

"I'm bound to make some at school," I'd said. "And then I could always pass Erri off as somebody's kid brother or cousin. I could have him here quite openly. He could leave with them through the front door, then I can smuggle him in again the back way, as I do now."

I'd been pleased with this idea. I couldn't think why Victoria and Robert looked so doubtful. It was surprising the difference the dark sky made. Somehow it didn't seem possible anymore. It seemed ridiculous.

When I went in to wake Erri, I found he was already up, standing by the window, looking out at the dark fir tree. I went over to him.

"What is it?" I asked. "What are you looking at?"

A silly question. I didn't blame him for not answering. The fir tree completely blocked the window. There was nothing else to see. I'd managed to get his window open at the top, and a few wet fronds dripped dismally onto the gray carpet.

"I'd better shut that," I said, and did so. Then I looked round, puzzled. "Erri, where's the knife? Don't spread your hands at me. The knife I used to chip away the old paint. I left it on the windowsill and it's gone." I saw his eyes flicker. "Don't lie, Erri. I know you've got it," I said.

After a brief hesitation, he went over to his bed, brought the knife out from under his pillow, and handed it to me.

"This knife? I put safe," he said virtuously.

"Erri! I'm not a fool."

He protested volubly in a mixture of his own language and English. I think he was trying to say that he'd thought I had left the knife there for him. "Present," he kept saying. "I think present like book, like choclat. Present for Erri." He looked at the knife wistfully and added, "Where I come from, all boy have knife. Is good."

"Is bad over here," I told him firmly. "In this country, only bad boys carry knives."

"Not carry," he said sulkily. "Put safe."

I suppose I should have told Victoria, but I did not take it seriously. It was only an old blunt fish knife, after all, not a dangerous weapon. Besides, it was my fault for leaving it there. He might well have thought I'd meant him to keep it.

The heavy rain had changed into the sort of fine drizzle that can soak you to the skin before you even notice.

"I wouldn't go out, Lesley," my aunt said. "It's a horrid day."

"I'll be all right. I'll wear my anorak. With the hood up," I added, seeing she still looked worried.

"You've only just gotten over hepatitis," my aunt

said. "It would be a pity to get pneumonia just now, don't you think?" She was so different from my mother. Mum would have told me I was to stay in and that was that, no argument, and we'd have had a row about it. I didn't know how to handle my aunt. Victoria rescued me, coming impatiently to the front door to see where I'd gotten to.

"Rain? It isn't raining," she told my aunt, ignoring the damp glitter in her hair and on her shoulders. "Besides, we're going to Shopping City, where it's all covered in. I'll look after Lesley and stop her from walking through puddles on the way to the bus shelter. You don't have to worry about her when she's with me. I'll see she doesn't get her feet wet."

It ended up with my aunt giving in. Before I left, she put some money into my hands, telling me to treat Victoria to lunch.

"But it's too much. I can't take all this," I protested.

"Why not? I want you to have it. If there's anything left over, buy yourself something."

I hesitated. "Mum told me not to be a burden to you."

She laughed and said, "You could never be that, my dear."

* * *

"How much did she give you?" Victoria asked, as soon as we were out of the house.

"Thirty pounds."

"*Thirty!* That's more than Mum ever gives me. Is she rich?"

"I don't know. I don't see how she can be. She works very hard and I don't suppose she makes much out of sewing, do you?"

"Anyway, it's rude to refuse a gift. She'd be hurt," Victoria said cheerfully. "If we just have a coffee and a bun for lunch, there'd be a lot left over. Still, it's up to you."

"If there's anything left over, we'll share it," I told her, and she smiled at me warmly.

"I'll get Erri for you," she offered. He was waiting for us in the garden shed, hunched up in his Save the Children anorak.

"Supposing she's in the kitchen? Supposing she sees you?"

"She won't. I'll do my commando stuff through the long grass."

The long grass must have been very wet. They came creeping back like drowned rats, but Erri was laughing. Victoria had made a game of it.

"We soldiers," he told me, and took my hand.

Once in Shopping City, he became very quiet. We had lunch first, hot chocolate, hamburgers and chips, and doughnuts. I was dividing the change into two piles when I noticed Erri watching me. So I made a third pile; ten pounds each for Victoria and me, and five pounds for Erri. He didn't say anything when I gave him the note. Just stared at it as if he wondered what I meant him to do with it.

"Come on, Erri. You must've seen money before," Victoria said. "Put it in your pocket and thank Lesley nicely."

"Thank you," he whispered.

As we walked through the store, he looked at everything with quick dark eyes. The piles of fruit in the market, the glittering shop windows with gold and silver watches, brightly colored clothes, life-sized toy dogs and miniature electric trains dazzled him. Victoria bought some pink leggings, and I bought a black T-shirt with a picture of a yellow camel on it, but he bought nothing. He seemed overawed.

"It's not surprising," Victoria said. "He probably came from some blood-stained country, with nothing but dust and guns . . . Nothing to hope for but a few handfuls of rice. It's no wonder he stares."

He did more than stare. He took. He filled his pockets. He must have done it a hundred times before, he was so quick, so skillful a little thief. We noticed nothing.

"Aren't you going to buy yourself anything,

Erri?" I asked, and he shook his head. I thought perhaps he wanted to save his money. Perhaps it made him feel rich. Secure.

Once out of Shopping City, however, he couldn't wait to show us how clever he'd been. The thin rain had stopped. A watery sunlight sparkled in the little yellow stones on the bracelet he held out to me.

"For you," he said, smiling. "And for you." He turned to Victoria and gave her a similar silver bracelet, only hers was studded with tiny rubies. Victoria took the bracelet from him without thanks and examined it carefully.

"Chips of glass," she said, "but it's real silver — look, there's the mark. Costume jewelry, but expensive enough. I think I know where it comes from. Erri, you never got these for five pounds."

He looked bewildered. He had been expecting praise. "You not like?" he said, sounding hurt, and then, as an idea struck him, he added quickly, "Is okay. I keep your money safe," and he brought out of his pocket the five-pound note I had given him and showed it to us with a proud smile.

17

Victoria took Erri by the arm and sat him down on the low wall surrounding a municipal flower bed full of red geraniums.

"Turn out your pockets," she said.

From where I sat, I could see one of the entrances to Shopping City. At any moment I expected someone to come running out, shouting, pointing at us. I thought we should have gone farther away, but Victoria said we'd only have farther to come back.

"We've got to return the things," she said. "Here, hold them, will you?"

It was a pathetic haul. Except for the bracelets, nothing was worth more than a pound or so: two bars of chocolate, a red ballpoint, chewing gum, a small rubber cat, a penknife . . . I remembered the fish knife he'd hidden under his pillow and wondered why I was so much more shocked at his stealing from a shop than from me — or rather from my aunt, for I'd taken the knife out of her kitchen drawer. If I'd made more of a fuss about it, he might not have stolen these things. I decided not to tell Victoria.

"What are you going to do?"

"Come and watch, if you like. Only keep well back. Pretend you're not with me, right? And hang on to Erri. Don't let him run off."

Erri didn't want to come, but I was curious. Holding him tightly, I followed Victoria back into Shopping City. When she turned into Swanley's we stopped just outside the open doorway and watched. She walked boldly up to the nearest counter and spread the small pile in front of an astonished assistant.

"These things belong to you," she said in her loud, confident Harwood voice. We could hear her quite plainly from where we stood. "I'm afraid my little cousin took them. He didn't realize what he was doing, of course. He's a kleptomaniac. It's very sad. The doctors say he may grow out of it, but at the moment we have to watch him like a hawk. Naturally we always return the things he takes."

With that, she turned and walked out, leaving the young salesgirl goggling after her. She passed us without giving us a glance. After a moment, we followed, trying not to run. I couldn't resist glancing back just before we were out of sight. The assistant had called another woman over, and they were talking excitedly. I didn't stay.

Victoria was waiting for us by the red geraniums. "Quick!" she said, and we fled down the pavement, dragging Erri between us.

Once we were safe on the bus again, we both lectured him. We told him it was wrong to steal. We told him he could've gotten us all into trouble. We told him what would happen to him if he did it again. "The police will catch you and send you back. You wouldn't like that, would you?"

He began to cry. Victoria told him we'd forgive him this time, but he wasn't to do it again. She took it much more calmly than I did.

"After all," she said later, "you can't really blame him for stealing. It's all right for us. We're given all the food we need, and all the clothes . . ." She broke off and looked down at the bag in her hands. "Pink leggings! I don't need pink leggings. I just wanted them. I don't suppose they'll even suit me. They'll make my legs look fat. Yet I wheedled you out of some of your aunt's money so that I could buy them. How can I be cross with Erri? Look how thin he is — and those scars! Think of what his life must've been like. No family, no home, just bombs and rubble. I bet he had to fight for every scrap of food, fight and steal and lie. I guess all the kids did. It was probably the only way they could stay alive, poor little devils."

I was sorry then. We did not go straight home when we got off the bus, but took him to the café in the park and bought him ice cream and a doughnut, as if trying to make up for all the meals he'd missed in his short life. Then we went to look for the soccer-playing boys, but they were not there today. So we played a few chasing games and hide-and-seek. (Victoria and I cheated at this. We did not want to risk losing Erri, so we peeked through our fingers when it was his turn to hide.) It was nearly suppertime when we got back. I said good-bye to Victoria and left Erri in the garden shed while I went to see if the way was clear.

Auntie Amy was in the kitchen, surrounded by bowls of fruit — strawberries, gooseberries, black currants — bags of sugar, and rows of empty jam jars. That was the second unlucky thing.

We ate our supper that evening in the formal splendor of the dining room, sitting side by side at one end of the long polished table; a cold supper — ham, salad, and raspberries and cream.

"I hope you had a good lunch, Lesley," my aunt

said, and I said it had been splendid, and Victoria had asked me to thank her (which she hadn't — we'd been too busy talking to remember to be polite).

"I meant to make the jam for the church bring-and-buy this afternoon," my aunt told me, "but one of my friends called in and we forgot the time. So I'll have to do it this evening."

I thought of Erri shut in the garden shed and wondered how long it would take her.

"I'll help you," I offered.

"That's kind of you, my dear, but I don't want you to get overtired."

"I won't. I'd like to help. It'll be fun."

Even with my help, it took so long. The fruit had to be hulled. She had only one saucepan suitable for making jam, so we had to do it in three lots, taking turns stirring the pink, frothing mixture with a long wooden spoon. I wondered if the hot, sweet smell was drifting out of the window and across the garden into the shed, where Erri crouched among the sacks of manure. Already the sky outside had turned deep blue.

"Is your wrist getting tired? Shall I take over the stirring?" my aunt asked. I handed her the spoon.

"It's so hot," I said. "My face is burning. I think I'll go and cool down in the garden for a moment."

The light from the kitchen window did not

reach the garden shed but patched the grass behind me with gold. I unlocked the door. It was dark inside. I heard Erri move, and whispered quickly, "It's all right. It's only me. My aunt's still in the kitchen. I'll have to wait now till she's in bed and asleep. She'd be bound to hear us if I tried to bring you in through the front door. I'll come for you as soon as I can."

"Okay," he said.

He sounded sleepy. I locked the door again and went back to the kitchen. My aunt was tilting a saucer on which was a little puddle of strawberry jam.

"There. That's done," she said.

"How can you tell?"

"Has your mother never made jam?" she asked. "No, I suppose she wouldn't. She was never one for cooking." She showed me how a skin had formed on the cooling jam in the saucer. It wrinkled when she tilted it. "That's how you tell," she said.

By the time we'd filled the jars with strawberry, then gooseberry, then black currant jam, it was dark outside, with a lopsided moon in the sky. The lights in the Harwoods' house went off one by one.

"I wish you'd go to bed, Lesley," my aunt said. "We've nearly finished now, and you must be tired. I'll just put the lids on and then I'll come up. Good night, my dear, and thank you for your help."

I went up to my room, put on my nightie and dressing gown, and waited on the second-floor landing. I heard her come up. I heard the doors opening and shutting: bedroom, bathroom, then bedroom again. Now silence. I gave her time to go to sleep, then I tiptoed down the stairs, unlocked the kitchen door, and went to fetch Erri from the shed.

It had been raining again. The ground was very wet. I had brought my small flashlight with me but did not switch it on until I was in the shed. Erri was sleeping, curled up on some sacks. He woke up with a cry when the light touched his eyelids, and I had to shine it quickly on my own face to reassure him it was me. He seemed nervous and bewildered.

As we crossed the garden, the light in the kitchen suddenly came on. I switched off my flashlight, and we both dropped down on our stomachs in the long grass. Through the stems I watched the light. After a minute or two, it went off again.

We waited, shivering. The grass was wet and the damp soaked through our thin clothes. The night air was cold. At last we got up and went to the kitchen door. It would not open. I turned the handle, first one way, then the other, and shook it. It was no good. We were locked out.

18

I stood in the Harwoods' garden in the cloudy moonlight, tossing gravel at Victoria's window and missing. The little stones hit the side of the house below her sill and fell soundlessly, harmlessly into the dark garden. Then Erri, whom I'd told to stay in the shed, came out of the shadows.

I did not see the size of the stone he threw, but it went straight and sure to Victoria's window and cracked the glass with a sharp sound that sent us scurrying away to hide in the bushes.

After a moment, Victoria's light went on. She came to the window, pushed it wide open, and leaned out. Seeing no other lights come on, we ran onto the lawn and waved frantically. She saw us and made a gesture with her hand, as if brushing us away. Although she said nothing and I could only see her as a silhouette, I somehow knew she was cross.

She pointed to our garden several times, then shut her window and turned off her light. We stood staring for a moment but nothing happened, so we climbed back over the wall and returned miserably to the garden shed, the damp sacks, and the spiders.

"We'll be all right," I whispered to Erri, putting my arm around him, trying to keep us both warm.

"She tell?"

"No. She'd never tell."

He was silent for a while. Suddenly he began wriggling. He was trying to take off his anorak.

"Erri! What on earth . . . ?"

"You haf. You cold," he said.

He was cold too. I could feel him shivering. I thought of the presents he had stolen for us, only to see them rejected. And now he wanted me to have his anorak. He wanted to give me something, not only to take. Somehow it made me feel happier about the lies we'd told for him, the way I had deceived my aunt. It seemed worth it now. "It's the best thing we've ever done," Victoria had said, and I believed it. I hugged him. He was the little brother I'd always wanted.

"You keep it. I've got my dressing gown."

"It wet."

"So's your anorak."

The door of the shed opened and a light shone

in our eyes, blinding us. "So there you are," Victoria said.

"You've come!"

"Of course. Isn't that what you wanted? You broke my window and danced about on the lawn, waving at me. I didn't think it was just high spirits in the middle of the night." She sat down on a sack of manure and switched off her flashlight. "So what's the matter? What are you doing here?"

"We're locked out." I told her what had happened. "It must've been my aunt," I said. "She must've come down again and checked the door. I don't know why."

"Forgot whether she'd locked it or not. Our grandmother is like that," Victoria said. "Always checking the gas taps. Go to the theater with her, and halfway through the first act, she'll say, 'I can't remember if I turned out my little electric fire. I think I'd better go back.' It used to drive Mum mad. This sack is damp!"

"They all are. What shall we do?"

"You'll have to sleep here," she told us. "It's no good thinking I can smuggle you into our house. Mum would be bound to hear us. She's restless tonight. Her light's still on. I saw it shining through the crack under her door as I tiptoed past. I guess she's reading. She usually does if she can't sleep. Trouble is, you can't trust her to stay put.

141

Sometimes she prowls about, going down to make herself a sandwich or fetch a book or something. I woke up the other night to find her sitting by my bed. Said she'd heard me talking in my sleep and had come in to see if I was all right. I took a risk coming out here tonight. I hope you appreciate it. What's that funny noise?"

"It's Erri's teeth chattering."

She put out her hand and touched our sleeves. "Good grief, you're both soaking wet. You are idiots." She thought for a moment, then sighed. "We'd better risk it. Come on," she said, and led us back over the garden wall and into their kitchen.

It was dark, but she did not switch on her flashlight. A little light came through the window, showing the dim shape of the table in the center, but leaving the terrible posters in shadow. Victoria lit all the gas rings and the oven. She gave us woolen sweaters out of the charity bags, so big that they came down past our knees. Then she put our wet clothes in the oven.

"Won't they scorch?"

"Not if we remember to take them out," she said.

She left the kitchen, telling us to be quiet as mice. "I won't be long," she said. "I'll just go and see if the enemy is still awake."

Left alone, we sat so still that the Harwood mice, venturing out of their holes in search of crumbs, made more noise than we did. We could hear the soft fluttering of the gas in the drafts and odd creaking sounds as the old house settled around us. Outside in the garden an owl cried, and I thought I heard footsteps, but nobody came.

Victoria was taking a long time. Erri had gone to sleep on a pile of old clothes. I watched the gaslight flicker over his face. He looked peaceful, sleeping on the floor in his enemy's kitchen, surrounded by invisible posters of war and famine and disaster. I suppose he had learned to sleep where he could: in the backs of trucks, in bombed houses, in barns. How different my life had been.

"Are you asleep?" Victoria whispered.

I jumped. I hadn't heard her come back. "No. I was thinking."

She sat down beside me. "What about?"

"Oh, about Erri. I used to feel sorry for myself because I never had a father when all my friends had. Erri's got nothing, not even friends to envy. Life isn't fair, is it? Is your mother still awake?"

"Her light's out. She must have gone to sleep. I've brought down my alarm clock. We'll have to be up before anyone else —"

"Victoria! How can I get back into my aunt's house? It's all locked up."

"I've been wondering about that. I've thought of a very clever way, but it depends on your front door. Is it just on a Yale lock or does your aunt bolt it at night?"

"She bolts it. And there's a mortise lock as well."

"Damn. No good pretending you just stepped out for the milk and it slammed shut behind you. What about windows, does she lock those?"

"Yes."

"What, every little one?"

"Yes. At least — there's a little round one in the downstairs bathroom that tilts open like a port-hole. The wood's warped. It won't even shut properly. But nobody would get through there."

"Not even Erri?"

We both looked at him, at the small tousled head, the narrow shoulders and delicate wrists.

"He might," I said. "But it's set high up in the wall. He'd need someone to lift him up."

"He's got us," she said.

"Shall we try now?"

"No, let him sleep, poor little squirt. I'll set my alarm for five. That'll give us plenty of time. We'd better try and get some sleep ourselves, I suppose, though I don't feel like it. I feel wide awake."

"So do I."

"Would you like some hot milk? We might as well make use of the gas rings."

We sat side by side in the flickering light of the gas stove, whispering like conspirators and drinking our hot milk. Above our heads, Kate Harwood slept. The enemy, Victoria had called her. Poor Call-me-Kate. I couldn't help feeling sorry for her. I wouldn't like to have Victoria for an enemy.

We'd been talking about my family. She wanted to know if I'd ever known my father or if he'd died before I was born. I told her I'd never had one, and she said I must have, biologically. I said, if so, somebody should've told my father, because he'd just walked out before I was born.

"I'm sorry," she said. "Would you rather not talk about it?"

I shrugged. "I don't mind. They say you can't miss what you've never known, and it's true. I didn't always envy my friends. Some of their dads I wouldn't have had as a gift. I used to look at them and think, 'Well, at least I wasn't stuck with you.' Mum and I are all right by ourselves. We get on fine."

She didn't say anything. I looked at her from under my lashes. Her face looked sad, bitter. I wondered if she was envying me my mother.

"I think my mum would have done just the same as yours," I said timidly, wanting to comfort her. "About Erri, I mean. She's terribly afraid of losing her job. And Auntie Amy would probably say the government must know best —"

"That's different! You don't understand," Victoria burst out. "If Mum had been ordinary, I don't think I'd mind so much. I mean, we all dither at times and worry about what people think and make mistakes. But she pretended she was something special. And she took me in. I thought she was wonderful. I adored her."

The owl called again outside the window, "Hoo! Hoo!" as if mocking her.

"How could I have been so stupid," Victoria muttered. "Do all kids think their mothers are perfect? Did you, when you were small?"

When I was small, I told her, my mother looked like a princess out of a fairy tale and smelled like a rose. I was proud of her when she took me to the play group and howled when she left me there, terrified in case she never came back. Sometimes she was late, and when she came at last and tried to take me in her arms, I'd hit her.

"I can remember screaming, 'I hate you! I hate you!' And I did for about a minute," I said. "Then I forgave her. I must have been about three."

"You think I'm behaving like a child?" she asked angrily.

"No. I forgave her, remember. Kids usually do."

She was silent, and I wondered if I'd offended her. Erri muttered and stirred in his sleep. She looked down at him.

146

"It's no good," she said. "I'm not a child any longer. I can't forgive her."

It was warm in the dark kitchen. She switched off the gas and we lay down side by side. I was getting sleepy now, but I wanted to hear what Victoria was saying, so I tried to keep awake. She was talking about her childhood. She'd begun collecting for charity when she was quite small, she told me, tottering behind her older brothers on her stumpy little legs, carrying an old lampshade nearly as big as herself.

"I loved it then," she said. "It made me feel important. And it was like a treasure hunt. When we got home, we'd sort everything out into piles and put price tickets on the good stuff. You've no idea what people give away — a black lace dress, a moth-eaten fur coat, a pair of red silk pajamas, nearly new, and extraordinary hats. We'd all dress up in them, Mum and Chris and Robbie and me. We'd parade about the kitchen, pretending to be the people they'd belonged to. You should've seen Chris in a feather hat and a silk dressing gown and high-heeled shoes, imitating Mrs. Featherstone-Harris. He's a marvelous mimic. He was much nicer then. He's changed. Why do people have to change? He's so stuffy now. He used to be fun."

"Did your father join in?" I asked her.

"No. Occasionally he'd come in early, and then

he'd watch us and laugh. But mostly he worked late. His job takes him away from home a lot. It was hard on Mum at first, I suppose, being alone with three kids. But now we're older and she's got all her charity committees, I don't suppose she minds."

"What's your father like?"

"You'll see for yourself on Friday. He's coming home. He rang up today to tell us, and we're all going to Heathrow to pick him up."

"Oh." My eyelids were getting heavy. I could hardly keep them open. I thought I heard Victoria say, "He's great. You'll like him. Everybody does. But be careful. You've got to remember he's one of the enemy." Then I fell asleep and dreamed I was lying in a stony desert under four flickering blue moons. All around me, the enemy crept and hid and rustled the paper in the crates.

19

At twenty past five the next morning, Erri and I were safe in our beds in my aunt's house. Nobody had seen us come in. The gardens had been veiled under a misty drizzle, the neighbors' curtains closed. Nobody had been awake to see Victoria and me lift Erri up to the small round window at the back. Victoria waited till he opened the door to let me in, then she went to her own bed.

I forgot to set my alarm. At eight o'clock, when Auntie Amy called up the stairs, "Lesley! Breakfast in fifteen minutes!" I did not even hear her. It was lucky I had shut and locked Erri's door, for she came up to my room. She did not wake me.

"You were sleeping so peacefully," she said when I came downstairs at last, "and it's such a horrid day. It seemed a pity to wake you."

It rained all day. I had no chance of getting Erri out into the garden shed and there seemed no point in it. We couldn't have gone out. He soon grew bored and restless. I was terrified my aunt would hear him. She was busy in her workroom on the floor below us, finishing by hand a trousseau for some rich lady. I put my radio on to mask any sounds we might make, but I couldn't relax.

Auntie Amy was puzzled that I chose to stay in my room, even when Victoria came. She offered us the sitting room with the television or the dining room with its big table for our drawings or games.

"You'd be so much more comfortable," she said.

"We like it up here," Victoria told her. "We have the whole floor to ourselves. Don't worry if you hear odd noises above your head. It'll only be us."

That night, Auntie Amy told me that she was going out the next day. She had finished the order she was working on and was taking it up to the shop in Kensington.

"I wondered if you'd like to come with me, Lesley? We could have lunch in the Dress Circle in Harrods and look around. It's a terribly expensive store, of course. Still, you might enjoy seeing it. It's so famous. And then we'll go and have tea with a friend of mine who lives near there. She said you'd be very welcome. Would you like that? Or have you made other plans?" she asked, as I hesitated.

"Victoria's coming over tomorrow," I lied. To-morrow was Friday, and Victoria would be going to Heathrow to meet her father. They were all going, she'd told me. It would be difficult for her to refuse.

"Perhaps she'd like to come with us to Kensington? I'm sure Isobel wouldn't mind an extra one for tea —"

"No, it's all right, thanks. She's going to take me to Golders Hill Park. They have animals there, deer and rabbits and peacocks, things like that." We both listened to the rain beating against the windows. "Or we might go to a movie in the afternoon, if it hasn't stopped raining by tomorrow. If that's all right?"

"Yes, of course," she told me. "I'm glad you and Victoria have become such friends. I feel I needn't worry when you're with her. I'm afraid I haven't been entertaining you as I should have, only I've been so busy. Never mind, now I've finished this order, we'll think of something nice to do. Perhaps, if the weather improves, you'd like to go to the seaside for a few days?"

I hoped the dismay I felt did not show on my face.

"I'd rather stay in London," I said. "Robert and Victoria will be going back to their schools in September, and Christopher's starting at Oxford. It'll be ages before I see them again. I mean, thank you very much, but you don't have to think of treats for me. I'm fine."

She smiled at me. "I'm glad you're happy here," she said. "I was afraid it would be so dull for you."

I had a feeling she was a little hurt, but there was nothing much I could do about it. I couldn't leave Erri on his own while I went jaunting off to the sea-side with her.

Auntie Amy had ordered a taxi for ten o'clock the next morning. The rain was falling heavily.

"You won't be able to go to Golders Hill Park," she said.

"It might clear up. And if it doesn't, we'll go to the movies. Don't worry about us. Look, here's your taxi! I'll help you carry your boxes down."

"You'll get soaked."

I put my anorak on and bundled my aunt and her parcels out of the house, down the steps, and into the taxi. Then I stood in the rain and waved her goodbye. Kind, gentle Auntie Amy. It was diffi-cult to believe she was one of the enemy. "But she is, Lesley," Victoria had said sternly. "You said yourself that you didn't think she'd help us hide Erri. Everyone who isn't our friend is our enemy, remember that. Like Mum. Like my father."

152

I turned and went slowly back into the house. Erri came flying down the stairs to meet me.

"She gone! She gone! Bad auntie gone!" he cried, prancing around me in high glee.

"She's not a bad auntie, why do you call her that?" I asked.

"She bad," he insisted. "Vicky tell me. She find me, she hit."

"She wouldn't!" I protested, but he skipped away and went running wildly through the house, upstairs and downstairs, shrieking with delight when I chased him. After three wet days imprisoned in his dark little room, the freedom went to his head. We had the whole empty house to play in — except Auntie Amy's workroom.

"Not in there!" I shouted, as he went toward it.

"Why not?"

"It's her workroom. Nobody's allowed in there. Not even me."

I was afraid he was going to disobey me. The key was on the outside. I turned it quickly and put it in my pocket.

"What in there?" he asked. "Monee?"

"No. A fierce dog."

"Dog? What dog?"

"Fierce. Like this." I growled and showed my teeth at him.

He laughed and went leaping downstairs again.

I wished he'd calm down, or that it would stop raining so that I could take him out and let him run and jump in the park where he couldn't break anything. He wanted to see the sitting room and the dining room, but that's where most of Auntie Amy's china children were.

I gave him lunch early, but he ate so quickly that it was soon over. He was always hungry. I handed him an apple and told him to see how slowly he could eat it, then looked out the window. The rain was beating down on the wet grass, forming puddles on the uneven path. It would be miserable out. I looked back at him: he smiled at me happily, chewing his mouthful of apple with exaggerated care. When he'd finished, I made him wash his face and hands, warned him not to touch anything, and took him into the sitting room to watch television. He looked round the room in much the same way he had looked at the glittering shop windows in Shopping City.

"Remember you mustn't touch," I warned him. "Not steal, understand? And if you break anything, I'll murder you."

He was looking now at the china figures. "Why children?" he asked.

"I suppose she likes children."

"She like haf me?"

I doubted it. "You're not made of china," I told

him. "She'd have to feed you and dress you and send you to school, and worry about you. She's old. These are easier."

He picked one up, a small boy in a blue smock and yellow trousers, holding a bird's nest, and made a face at it.

"Careful!" I said.

For a moment I thought he was going to throw it across the room, but if he'd been tempted, he changed his mind and put it down again. He looked at the television, which I'd switched on, but he kept fidgeting, swinging his legs, wriggling on the couch, turning to look out of the window at the rain.

I tried all the programs, but nothing held his interest for long.

"Would you rather go out?" I asked at last.

He glanced at the window again. "Rain," he said sulkily.

"We could take an umbrella."

"Take? Where we take?"

"Just for a walk." I would be glad to go out. Or at least back upstairs. I was terrified he would break something down here. He wouldn't keep still. Lying on the couch, he kept waving his feet in the air, bouncing up and down on the cushions; now he was trying to turn a somersault.

"Careful!" I cried.

Too late. One of his feet caught the small table beside the couch and tipped it over. The bird's-nest boy and a china girl with a bird fell to the floor. The carpet was soft, but luck was against us: both figures broke. The china girl lost the hand holding the bird. The china boy lost his head.

I lost my head too.

"You stupid little nit!" I shouted at the top of my voice. "Look what you've done now! I could kill you!"

He looked terrified. I caught hold of him as he ran for the door, and he started screaming, wriggling so much that I was afraid his thin wrist would break in my hands. When I let go, he hit out at me with his hard little fists, catching me painfully on my cheekbone and in my left eye.

I put both my arms around him and hugged him to me tightly, so that he couldn't move. "It's all right. It's all right, Erri. I won't hurt you even though you've hurt me. Look at my poor eye! But I'm not making a fuss, am I? Oh, shut up, won't you! Stop that horrid noise! Somebody'll hear you and call the police or something and then we'll be in trouble."

I shouldn't have mentioned the police. He started screaming, "No! No! No!" louder than ever. I was afraid the whole street would hear him and come running to see who was being murdered.

"Shut up! Please shut up," I begged. "You can have a chocolate cookie. You can have the whole packet." He was sobbing now, great gasping sobs as if he'd used up all his breath in screaming. A chocolate cookie would probably choke him. I didn't think he'd heard what I'd said. His eyes normally brightened when you said the word chocolate, but they were screwed up now, leaking tears through his glistening black lashes. His whole face was wet, and his nose was running, and he shook and shuddered in my arms so much that I thought he'd fall apart. He looked terrible.

I wished my mother were there. I wished my aunt would come back. I wished Victoria hadn't gone to Heathrow. I thought Erri was having a fit, and I didn't know what to do.

I sat on the couch with Erri on my lap and rocked him in my arms, backward and forward, backward and forward, while he shuddered and snuffled and soaked my shirt with his tears.

Then the doorbell rang.

20

Christopher Harwood stood on the doorstep, hunched in a black leather jacket, his fair hair darkened by the rain.

"Well, let me in," he said impatiently, as I stood and stared at him. "It's wet out here, in case you hadn't noticed."

"I thought you'd gone to Heathrow to pick up your father," I said, not moving out of his way. I had shut the sitting-room door behind me, telling Erri to stay out of sight, but there was no depending on it.

"Well, I haven't, as I would have thought was obvious," Christopher said, pushing past me into the hall. He took off his heavy jacket, looked round, and, seeing nowhere to put it except a spindly gilt chair, dropped it on the floor. "Robert and Vicky have gone with Mum, so I backed out. I thought it was a good chance to talk to you about that boy, before Dad gets back. I suppose he's up in his room? Let's go in here —"

"No!" I said, but it was too late. He'd opened the sitting-room door and was in before I could stop him. I expected some sort of outcry, a scuffle of running feet, even the sound of blows. But there was nothing.

"Come on," Christopher said. "Don't just stand there. We might as well make ourselves comfortable while we talk. Hey, what's this on the floor? Broken china. Part of your aunt's famous collection, by the look of it. Did you knock the table over? No wonder you've been crying."

"I haven't been crying," I said. I looked round the room. Erri was nowhere to be seen.

"Funny. Your eyes are all wet and bloodshot, at least one of them is. And you've got a bruise coming up on your cheek. Have you been fighting? Was it that boy?"

"No! I — I tripped and fell into this table," I said, picking it up and setting it on its feet. "Caught my face on the edge. That's how the china got broken."

Christopher was kneeling on the floor, the pieces of Auntie Amy's ruined children in his hands. He looked up at me and said admiringly,

"That was well thought up, on the spur of the moment. What's the boy doing hiding behind that blue chair over there? I can see his feet —"

Erri burst out from behind the chair and raced for the door. But though he was quick, Christopher was quicker. He fielded Erri as neatly as if he were a softball and held him firmly in his hands while the small boy wriggled and yelled.

"What a horrible noise. What shall we do with him, Lesley? Dunk him in a bath of cold water, that might calm him down. Don't kick me, you little wretch. Nobody's going to hurt you. Talk about a tantrum! What brought it on?"

"He was afraid he'd be blamed for breaking the china figures. But it was my fault, not his. Erri, nobody's going to blame you."

Erri looked at me but didn't answer. He was quiet now and seemed subdued.

"If you're a good boy, we'll give you some cake," Christopher said. "First wipe your nose. You look a right mess. Have you got a hanky?"

Erri sniffed and shook his head.

"Never mind. I've got one somewhere. Now where did I put it?"

But Erri was gone, quick as a blink. He leaped for the door, throwing the little table to the floor again, and raced across the hall. The fallen table impeded us. By the time we reached the hall, the front door was open and Erri was bounding down the steps. His foot slipped on the wet stone, and he fell.

"He's dead!" I cried, but the dead are silent. Erri lay on the streaming pavement, his head resting against the stone wall, and whimpered like a sick puppy. As we ran down toward him, he moved, tried to get up, and yelped with pain.

Christopher knelt beside him. "Can you move your foot? Where does it hurt? Let me see . . ."

Erri winced and pushed his hand away. A cut or graze on his shoulder was bleeding; the blood, thinned by the rain, ran down his arm in pink ribbons. His forehead was mottled with dark bruises, and his trousers were torn.

"It's his ankle. We'd better get him out of this rain or he'll get pneumonia on top of everything," Christopher said.

He lifted Erri and carried him carefully up the wet steps and into the house. As I followed him, I looked over my shoulder and saw the Harwoods' car drawing up outside the house next door. Call-me-Kate was driving. I didn't stop to see who was sitting beside her, but shot through the door, slamming it behind me.

I had no idea whether we'd been seen or not.

Erri's ankle was badly swollen. There was no gauze in Auntie Amy's first-aid box, only Band-Aids and antiseptic cream, so we bandaged it with a cotton scarf of mine, soaked in cold water. We bathed the graze on his arm and washed away the dark smudges from his forehead, all of which proved to be mud except one small bruise over his left eye. Then we put him to bed in his little room, and I went down to make him a mug of hot chocolate, leaving him to face Christopher's questions. Poor Erri, what else could I do?

I had trained him well, however. When I came back carrying the tray with mugs of hot chocolate and slices of cherry cake, I found Christopher looking exasperated.

"Whatever I ask him, he keeps saying he can't remember," he said. "He says he had an accident and can't remember anything. Somehow I just don't believe him. He comes out with it too pat."

I put the tray down on the table and looked at Erri. His dark eyes were watchful and sly. "I don't think he trusts you," I said. "He thinks you'll betray him."

Christopher flushed. "*Betray!* Do you have to use such emotive language? You know, I sometimes wish I was still a child. It's easy for you and Vicky. Everything's so simple and dramatic when you're a kid. Even Robert won't use his brain. Don't you realize you're not helping him? He must have friends somewhere, relatives perhaps. We should've tried to find them." He turned back to Erri. "Who looked after you, Erri? Who were you with before you met us?"

"I can't remember. I had bad accident. I can't remember this."

"Erri!" I said reproachfully, but it was no good. He would not tell us where he came from. At each question, he slid a little further down into his bed until only his black eyes showed above the blanket, all the while repeating like a parrot, "I can't remember. I had bad accident. I can't remember this."

"Somebody taught him to say that," Christopher said. "I'll bet you anything he's been taught to say that." I kept quiet, and he went on, "There was nothing in the papers about those people at Heathrow, you know. Not even a paragraph. I looked. Why did I ever let Vicky and Robert get me into this mess?"

We drank our hot chocolate in silence. I took Erri's empty mug away and settled him down in his bed. He smiled at me sleepily. Christopher said his family would be back from Heathrow any minute — "If they're not home already."

So he hadn't seen the car, I thought. Perhaps they hadn't seen him either. It didn't matter if they'd only seen me. I glanced at my watch.

"What's the time?" Christopher asked.

"Half-past four."

"When are you expecting your aunt back?"

"She said she'd be back about six."

"We ought to talk," he said, and sighed.

Erri's eyes were shut. He was already asleep, long before his normal bedtime. It had been a hard day for him, what with one thing and another. But I was surprised that he could sleep, not knowing what was going to happen to him, not knowing what Christopher would do.

"Poor kid," Christopher said softly. "I'll have to tell Dad about him, you know. If not today, then tomorrow. Come on, let him sleep. I'll mend the china for you before I go. It won't take long."

Before I left the room, I glanced back and thought I saw Erri's eyelids flicker. I waited a moment but they did not open, so I shut the door softly and locked it.

I sat on the other side of the kitchen table watching Christopher stick the head back on the bird's-nest boy. "I wish Erri was as easy to fix as this," he said. "Don't look at me like that. I know you and Vicky think I'm a cold-hearted monster, but I have to do what I think is right. For Erri, not only for us."

"You promised," I said.

"Only conditionally. Dad will know what to do. He may not be into charity the way Mum is, but he does what he can. And he's sensible."

"Sensible!" I repeated, and he told me sharply that there was nothing wrong with being sensible.

"Why don't you try it?" he asked. "Can't you see Erri needs help, more help than we can give him? Just look at yourself in the mirror. You've got a black eye coming up. He must've hit you really hard, and you're his friend."

"He was frightened."

"I know. I'm not blaming him, poor little devil. It's just — well, if you ask me, he needs special care. From people who're trained to deal with cases like his. Dad would know how to get the right help. Be sensible, Lesley. You know you can't keep him forever. What are you waiting for?"

Be sensible, Lesley. How could I be? How could I betray Erri? It would break my heart.

I tried to think of a plan, but my head ached. Five days for a letter to reach Mum in Cairo. I could telephone her . . . she would never understand. She didn't know Erri. She'd think I'd gone mad. She'd think it was like the puppy I wanted, though I knew we weren't allowed pets in our apartment. When I cried, she gave me a new bicycle. What would she buy me to forget Erri?

"Give me a little more time to think of something," I said.

He sighed. "I'll give you till tomorrow," he told me, and would not change his mind.

"I'm sorry, Lesley," he said. "I really am."

When Christopher left, I looked at the bird's-nest boy and the girl who went with him. You could hardly see the scars round the neck and wrist where they'd been glued. Only if you looked very closely. Should I tell my aunt I'd broken them or leave her to find out one day? She might not notice for years. I might be back in Devon by then, and she and Erri only memories . . .

I wanted to smash the simpering china boy. I wanted to smash them all, her pretty china children, and give her Erri to take their place. He would fill her empty house better than they did.

Perhaps she'd think so too. After all, I'd never given her a chance. If I asked her, if I explained . . . I put the bird's-nest boy back on his table in the sitting room. Sitting down on the sofa, waiting for my aunt to come back, I began to dream. When you're desperate, you're prepared to try anything.

21

It was nine o'clock before I could get myself to ask her. I knew it was hopeless before I began. She looked delicate and old in her gray silk blouse and amber beads, sitting on her favorite armchair with her china children arranged neatly about the room.

I thought of Erri, his hair ragged from where Victoria had cut it with blunt scissors, his feet bare, racing up and down the stairs, shrieking with wild laughter. I remembered how often he woke in the night, crying out from a nightmare, and sat bolt upright in bed, refusing to go to sleep again. I remembered how he'd lied to us and offered us stolen gifts. I thought of the scars on his back and Christopher saying, "If you ask me, he needs special care, people who are experienced in cases like his." My eye was still sore from where he'd hit out at me in terror.

How could I expect Auntie Amy to look after him? She was not used to real children.

"Lesley, what's happened to your face?" she'd asked when she saw me. "Has somebody hit you? Not Victoria!"

"No, not Victoria," I agreed. "I wasn't looking where I was going. I walked into a tree."

She believed me. She always believed me. It never seemed to occur to her that I might be lying. She trusted me. It made me feel bad, so when she asked me if I'd enjoyed the film, I told her the truth.

"I didn't go. Victoria went with her mother and Robert to Heathrow after all. Christopher called round to tell me. He didn't offer to take me to the film in her place. I suppose it never occurred to him. He thinks I'm just a silly kid."

"Poor Lesley. So you've been all by yourself," she said. "Never mind. We must try and think of a treat for you tomorrow. What would you like to do?"

A treat! Tomorrow Christopher would tell his father and it would all be over. Unless I could stop him . . . My aunt was smiling at me kindly. I had a sudden bright vision of her standing by my side, the two of us facing Christopher and his father together, and my aunt saying in her gentle voice, "A runaway boy? No. There's nobody like that here. There's only my adopted son Erri."

She was my last chance.

"I'd like — I want to tell you something. About a boy."

"A boy?" she repeated, and looked a little startled. I could almost see the thoughts running through her head — she's too young to have a boyfriend . . . of course, they do start earlier nowadays, I'm told . . . surely not Christopher Harwood. He's too old for her . . .

"A small boy," I said. "About seven or eight, that's all. His name is Erri."

"Erri? That's an unusual name. How do you spell it?" she asked.

As if it mattered how you spelled it! People are extraordinary, the things they think important.

"I don't know. We never asked him. With one or two r's, I imagine," I told her.

"I'm sorry, dear. I just wondered. Go on."

"He — he hasn't got anyone to look after him. His mother's dead and, as far as we can gather, he never had a father. Like me —" I shouldn't have said that. She didn't have to be sorry for me. I had Mum, and that was good enough for me. I didn't miss the father I'd never known. But it had made me feel closer to Erri, as if he really were my brother. "He's got nobody, only us —"

"Us?" she asked as I broke off. "You mean —

do the Harwoods know about him, then? Is he one of their charities?"

"No! He's not! They don't know anything about him. It's nothing to do with them," I cried, remembering my promise to Christopher to keep them out of it. Though why I should keep my promise when he was planning to break his, I don't know.

"Who's looking after him?" she asked.

"Nobody."

"Somebody must be, Lesley, a boy of that age —"

"They beat him and terrified him. His back's covered with scars."

"Oh!" She drew in her breath, her face crinkling with distress.

"So he ran away," I said. "Can he stay here? Please! He's got nowhere else to go. Please, Auntie Amy, let him stay. After all, you like children, you collect them —" I gestured toward the china figures. "He's better than they are. He's *real!*"

"Lesley —"

"Erri needs someone badly and I'm too young. They wouldn't let me adopt him," I said, and began to cry.

She put her arm around me and murmured, "It's all right. It's all right, Lesley. I'll do what I can, I promise. There must be people who can help. Mrs. Harwood might be able to tell us —"

170

"No!" I cried.

"But, Lesley, she knows about that sort of thing —"

"She doesn't know anything. Anyway, she's a fraud. She wouldn't help. She's afraid of getting into trouble."

She looked at me in surprise. "I don't understand," she said slowly. "Lesley, what is all this? How do you know she won't help? You say she doesn't know about the boy —"

"No, and I don't want her to. Why can't you look after him?" I demanded. "You could adopt him. She's already got three children. You haven't got any."

She looked away from me. I wanted to say sorry but I couldn't. I was afraid of crying again. After a long moment, she said briskly, "I'm too old. I couldn't adopt a child now even if I wanted to, and I don't. It's probably just as well. I'm not very good at looking after children, am I?"

I didn't answer. What could I say?

"Now you'd better tell me about this little boy. Erri, didn't you say? I may not be able to adopt him, but that doesn't mean I can't help. I both can and will, my dear. Where is he now, by the way?"

She was waiting for an answer, and I couldn't think. My mind suddenly blanked out, as it does sometimes at school when we're doing math. "He's . . . he's . . . he's in hiding somewhere," I said at last.

"Where?" When I didn't answer, she stared at me. "Lesley, not here? In my house?"

I nodded.

"You'd better take me to him," she said gently. "I think I should meet my guest, don't you? Don't look so worried, my dear. I won't wake him if he's asleep. I just want to see him with my own eyes, to make certain that he's really there."

Did she think I'd made it all up, that Erri was only a sick fancy of mine? Well, she was wrong. It's true I'd half thought so once, when I first saw his face at the window, but I had been still weak then, pale and feeble. Now I had changed.

There was nobody in the room I had locked. The light was on. Above our heads, the naked bulb swung gently, scattering shadows over the empty bed. The window was wide open at the bottom. The fir tree that had pressed against the glass now edged its dark fingers over the sill. Erri had gone.

I ran to the window and looked down through the branches. On the pavement far below, I saw Victoria and Robert standing in the rain, look-ing up.

"He's on the roof," Victoria shouted. "Throw his mattress down! And pillows! Anything soft! Christopher's ringing the fire brigade."

My aunt was beside me at the window. We both leaned out and looked up. I could see Erri's legs hanging over the edge of the roof a little way past the tree. The makeshift bandage had come loose on his ankle and was blowing in the wind. I could hear the gutter creaking, and Erri whimpering with fear.

My aunt was dragging the mattress off the bed now, her back to me. I climbed quickly out of the window.

The tree enclosed me in soft, dripping foliage. Its thin branches broke off in my hands, dipped under my weight, parted, and let me through. I was falling . . . I just had time to think that I'd made a terrible mistake and was going to die for it. Then something hit me in the back and I found myself lying in a rough hammock of interlaced branches, looking up through the green needles at the darkening sky.

For a moment I was too frightened to move. Then I heard someone calling my name, my aunt or Victoria, not Erri. I turned my head carefully and saw that the trunk of the tree was within reach, thin enough for my hands to grasp securely, thick enough to bear my weight. I moved my arm slowly, feeling my leafy hammock rock beneath me. Water fell on me from the branches above, and the trunk tilted like the mast of a ship at sea.

I had always loved climbing trees, and now that my strength was back, I hadn't expected to be frightened. But I had never climbed a fir before, nor been so near the top of any tree. The branches crowded me, getting in my way, growing out thin and sharp, like the prickles of a hedgehog. I had to force my way through them, my feet slipping on the wet wood, my hands clinging to the narrowing trunk so hard that the pattern of the bark printed itself on my palm. And at every move, the whole tree dipped and groaned and trembled under my weight.

Through the foliage I could see Erri on the edge of the roof. The nearest branch was out of his reach and looked too thin to bear even his light weight. He must have climbed up close to the trunk, as I was doing, and crawled his way along the gutter until he lost his nerve. Perhaps he had looked down and seen how far it was to fall.

I didn't call out for fear of startling him. I didn't think he had seen me. His head was turned the other way. Something about the way he tilted it made me think he was listening. I listened too. I heard the wind in the branches, the rain dripping and my own breathing. Then, far in the distance, I heard the sound of a siren. Immediately, as if this was what he had been waiting for, Erri drew his feet up into the gutter, wriggled round so that he was facing the roof, and began to climb on all fours up the steep slope.

I watched in horror, afraid to move, afraid even to breathe in case I disturbed him. He was halfway up before his bare foot slipped on the shining tiles. For a moment, he lay full length, his fingers scrabbling uselessly, then he began to slide backward toward the edge of the roof.

As if in a dream, it seemed to happen in slow motion. I had time to fling myself upward and sideways, so that my weight pulled the top of the tree beneath him, just before he fell. He came crashing through the thin branches. I caught hold of a fistful of T-shirt with my free hand and pulled him toward me. I heard the cotton rip, but the slight check had given him the chance to catch hold of a thicker branch and swing himself onto the trunk just below me.

"Hold on!" I cried.

He clung with arms and legs to the trunk of the tree and rested his wet face against its rough bark. I climbed carefully past him and, standing on a lower branch, put my arm around him and held him safe. Below us, I could see a blue light winking.

I told him that I would be his sister, whatever happened, that even if he had to go into a home, I wouldn't forget him. I'd write to him every week, I said. I'd visit him whenever I could. I'd ask Mum if he could spend his holidays with us. I'd remember his birthdays, if he'd tell me the date. I'd help him if he was ever in trouble . . .

I don't know whether he heard me or not. He was looking past me, his wide, dark eyes reflecting the flashing blue light below. "Not police! It for fire! It not police, Lesley," he said, and smiled.

A small crowd had gathered on the wet pavement. The Harwoods were there and my aunt. I thought she was crying, but perhaps it was only the rain in her eyes. There were people from neighboring houses who had come out to watch, and a boy on a bicycle who had stopped on his way home. They all cheered as the firemen brought us down.

22

The fireman's red face beamed down at me like an enormous sun.

"It's usually cats we're asked to fetch down from trees, not young girls," he said. "Odd idea to go climbing in the dark."

"Her little brother got out onto the roof. She saved his life," someone told him.

"Brave girl, brave girl." Another face, one I didn't recognize, peered down at me. "Are you all right? Nothing broken?"

"The doctor's coming," Victoria said.

"Victoria!"

The strange face went away and was replaced by Victoria's. She knelt down beside me. I was lying on Auntie Amy's sofa where the fireman had put me. "I'm sorry," I said. "I'm sorry." I tried to sit up but she pushed me down onto the cushions again. "Is Erri hurt?" I asked.

"What are you apologizing for? Erri's all right. You saved his life. Mum's got him cornered in your blue armchair. He won't get away till she's got him all sorted out and organized. Oh, Lesley, you should've seen her face when she saw him! She knew at once who he must be."

"Was she angry?"

"Not angry, no, more sort of . . . stricken, that's the word."

"Stricken?"

"As if she was thinking, 'How could they do this to me? How could my whole family deceive me so?' For a moment I thought she'd crumble, that she'd never be the same person again. You know, I was almost frightened. It would've been like the house collapsing around us. But I needn't have worried. The next moment she was organizing everything. Enjoying herself, probably. She doesn't care what we think."

She was talking rapidly and seemed lit up by a sort of nervous excitement. I felt too dazed to take everything in. There were too many people in the room. At times the noise of their voices in the room blurred and receded, then came back louder than ever. My aunt was talking to the firemen, shaking hands with them as they left. I could hear Call-me-Kate's voice announcing, as if to a large audience, "He won't be long," and for a moment I caught sight of her face.

"She's not enjoying herself," I said. "She looks awful."

"She'll never forgive me," Victoria said.

A man, a complete stranger, was standing in the middle of the room, looking at me thoughtfully.

"Who's that man?" I asked.

"That's Dad," Victoria said.

Her father was not as tall as I had expected, not even as tall as Christopher, but somehow he stood out. He looked so sure of himself, so powerful. His eyebrows were thick and dark like Robert's, his brown eyes deceptively mild.

"Don't let Christopher talk to him," I whispered.

"It's too late, Lesley," Victoria told me. "Mum's not a fool, and Chris has already been talking. It'll all have to come out now."

"But I promised —"

"We all promised Erri things. We should've listened to Dad. He's always warned us to be careful of promises."

"What will happen now?"

She didn't answer. The voices had died away. I looked across the room and saw that the blue chair was empty and most of the people had left. There was only Mr. Harwood, standing in the middle of the room as if waiting for something.

"Where's Erri?" I asked.

"Don't worry, my dear," my aunt said. Victoria

had faded away, and my aunt was kneeling beside me in her place. "Erri's in bed in the spare room next to yours, the big one, not the small one he was in. The doctor is with him, and Mrs. Harwood. I don't think there's anything seriously wrong, but it's best to be careful. I think the doctor will give him something to make him sleep. Now we must get you to your room. Mr. Harwood's going to carry you up."

"No."

"Yes," Mr. Harwood said firmly. "The doctor wants to see you before he goes, and doctors like their patients to be in bed looking suitably ill when they come to see them. Otherwise they get annoyed with the person who called them out. In this case, me. Your aunt is coming with us. You needn't be afraid I'll kidnap you," he added, smiling.

He spoke kindly. He was treating me like a child.

"I can walk."

"Let's see you stand up before we decide, shall we?"

I got up from the sofa and immediately felt dizzy. Mr. Harwood lifted me off my feet without a word and carried me upstairs.

"You're heavier than you look," he said, puffing a little when he reached my room. "Or I'm out of condition."

"Did you carry Erri up too?"

"The boy? No, my wife did. With Victoria watching like a hawk to see she didn't drop him. You needn't worry. He's quite safe."

"For how long?" I asked.

He looked down at me. I think the bitterness in my voice surprised him. He was used to people liking him. I expected him to brush my question aside, but he answered seriously, "I don't know the facts, of course, only what I've been able to gather from a no doubt garbled version, but I would be extremely surprised if there was any question of the boy being sent back against his will, especially if there is the slightest danger to him. It would depend on the conditions in the country he comes from, of course, and whether he has any relatives there, or if satisfactory arrangements can be made to receive him —"

"You mean you can't promise anything."

"Lesley!" my aunt said. I suppose I had sounded rude. I mumbled an apology.

"I can promise you one thing," he said slowly. "I will do everything I can for the boy, and I'm not entirely without influence." He smiled down at me and added gently, "You can trust me, really you can."

"I only wish you'd felt you could trust me," my

aunt said. Somehow, although she didn't sound re-proachful, it made me feel bad.

"That's all very well," Victoria said when I told her. She had come in to see me after the others had gone downstairs. "We may know we can trust them to do what they think best. But their idea of best is not necessarily the same as ours. Your eyes look funny. Are you going to sleep?"

"No."

"You look as if you are. I suppose the doctor gave you something?"

"They made me take it. Don't go, Vicky —"

"I have to. I promised your aunt I wouldn't stay long. Besides, they're all talking downstairs and I want to know what's happening."

"Vicky, what will they do? They'll take Erri away from us, won't they? Even if they don't send him back, they'll take him away."

"We always knew we couldn't keep him," she said gently. "He had to go one day. He's not a pet. He doesn't belong to us."

"I wanted him to belong. I wanted him to be my brother." I tried to raise my head off the pillow but it was too heavy. "I want to come down with you. I want to know what happens."

My brain was so fogged with sleep that I could

182

hardly see Victoria, but her clear Harwood voice reached me through the mists.

"You will," she said, "because I'll tell you all about it. I'll try and remember every word for you. You know, it's funny. I've never had a friend I could tell everything to before."

"Nor have I." My voice was indistinct. I don't know if she heard me. But I heard her.

"Don't worry," she said fiercely. "I'll fight for Erri, and so will Robert. And tomorrow you can help us again. We won't let them send him out of reach. We're not going to lose him forever."

Victoria and Robert came over the next day. I hadn't missed anything, they told me. The grown-ups had been too interested in Erri to have time for them. My aunt, their mother, and Christopher had taken turns sitting by his bed that night.

"We offered to help, but they wouldn't let us. And Dad didn't want to discuss anything. He was tired, he said. He was going to bed. He had had a long day. But he had time to talk to Chris. *Chris!* From what you told us, it was Chris's fault that Erri tried to run away. I'll never forgive him for that."

"He couldn't know Erri wasn't really asleep. You've got an unforgiving nature," Robert told her. "It's a flaw in your character. You ought to do something about it. You ought to practice forgiving people. Don't you think so, Lesley?"

"Yes," I said.

Victoria looked as if I'd stabbed her in the back, and I wondered if I was going to be added to her list of the unforgiven. But I had seen Call-me-Kate earlier that morning, coming down from Erri's room. She'd stopped and asked me how I was and said I was a brave girl. Though she smiled at me, I thought she looked dreadful. Her voice had lost its confident ring, and the color in her rough red cheeks had faded. She was tired, of course, having sat up half the night, but it was more than that. Something had gone out of her. She looked desperately unhappy.

"I think you should start by forgiving your mum," I said.

"Why don't you mind your own business!" Victoria shouted. So much for having found a friend to whom one could tell anything.

She came back after tea. She had brought some coloring books for Erri, so I took her up to see him. He was lying like a young prince in his comfortable bed in the room that had once been my mother's and Auntie Amy's nursery. He saw Victoria's eyes go to the bars on the window and said, smiling at us, "Lesley's auntie sleep here when baby. Now I live here. Is my room."

"Doesn't he know he can't stay here?" Victoria asked, when we'd left him with his coloring books.

"I don't know. I haven't said anything. Let them tell him."

"Poor Erri. He'll never forgive us when he finds out. Dad's been on the telephone all morning, talking to the Immigration people —"

"They're not going to send him back?"

"No. They wanted him to go into care right away, but Dad talked them out of that. They've agreed to leave him here until suitable foster parents can be arranged, but it won't be for long. They've already got someone in mind. Lesley, guess what? Mum offered to adopt him, but Dad said it was out of the question. Why on earth do you think she did that?"

"To make up for letting you down," I said.

"Do you really think so?"

"Yes."

She was silent for a moment, then she said with an effort, "I was wrong and you were right. I forgive her. After all, nobody's perfect."

"Will you tell her?"

"That I forgive her? How can I? Besides, I think

she's avoiding me. She keeps rushing around, help-ing your aunt, ringing up people she knows in Wel-fare, talking to Dad, sorting out clothes for Erri. Even if I could pin her down, I can't just walk up to her and say, 'I forgive you, Mum.' She'd think I was mad. What do you think, Robbie," she asked, as Robert came in, having been sent up by my aunt. "Shall I tell Mum I've forgiven her?"

"I would just be nice to her. She'll get the idea soon enough," he advised. "Let the whole thing blow over. We've been lucky so far. They've been too busy to pay much attention to our misdeeds. You don't want to tempt fate."

"What do you think, Lesley? What would you do?"

"I'd tell her straight out," I said, "and get it over with."

So that's what she did. She walked straight up to her mother and said, "I forgive you, Mum." And instead of putting her in her place, as some moth-ers would have done, Kate burst into tears and took Victoria into her arms.

23

It is winter now. The young Harwoods are away at boarding school and college, and I am at Redwood Comprehensive. I have made new friends, but it's not the same.

"Good," I said when Erri left. "Nobody's going to wake us up in the middle of the night anymore. Our life's our own again."

My aunt wasn't fooled. She knew I missed him. I think she had grown fond of him during the time he was with us, but she was always nervous. She insisted that I get her up whenever he woke from a nightmare, though he only wanted me and would push her away rudely. He had found out that he was not going to be allowed to stay. He blamed her for it, not Mr. Harwood, whom he liked, or the government, of which he'd never heard. It was hard on her when she was always so kind.

Victoria said my aunt had spoiled him, that was

the trouble. "Mum would've been better. She'd soon have had him shaking collection boxes with the rest of us."

She and her mother are friends now. But that isn't the same either. They seem too careful with each other. Too polite. But Robert says that will wear off in time.

"They'll be better in the end, you'll see," he said. "Vicky's growing up, like me. You begin to see things differently then, especially your parents. Everyone changes."

"Have I changed?" I asked.

He looked at me. "Yes. You're prettier."

"No, seriously. Am I more sensible? More mature?"

"You would be, if you stopped moping about Erri. He'll be all right."

My aunt, too, comforted me. "Erri's only a short train journey away," she told me. "Half an hour at most. You'll be able to visit him once he's settled down. Meanwhile you can always write to him."

"He can't read."

"Mrs. Chester will read his letters to him until he learns to read for himself. And I'm sure she'll write back for him. They're nice people, Lesley. He'll be happy with them."

They *were* nice people, his new foster parents. I had seen them. The first time Erri was taken to visit them, he hadn't wanted to go and had cried at the last minute, clinging to me. So Miss Halley, the social worker, asked me if I'd come too, and I'd agreed. I sat in the back of her car with my arm round Erri as we drove through the gray streets into the greener suburbs.

"Look, there's a pond with boys fishing!" I said. "We're practically in the country. Do you like the country, Erri?"

"No," he said.

"It isn't really the country, Erri," Miss Halley assured him. "This is just a park."

"You'll be able to fly kites here, Erri," I told him, but he said sulkily, "Not like."

"Oh, don't be such a misery!" I cried angrily. I thought the social worker would tell me off, but she pretended not to hear.

"I was going to buy you one of those dragon kites for Christmas," I went on, "so we can fly it together when you visit us. But of course, if you don't want one —"

"They not let me!" he whispered fiercely.

"Won't let you fly a kite?"

"Not let me come."

"Of course they will," I said, but he shook his head. He was trembling again.

"I think we should go back now," I told the social worker. "Erri doesn't want to stay with them."

"We're only going there to tea," she said. "I thought I'd explained. There is no question of Erri staying with them today. This is just a first meeting to see how they take to each other. Don't worry, Erri. If you find you're not happy with them, then we'll think of something else."

"I stay in Lesley's house," he said, but she told him gently that that was impossible.

We drove on in silence. Finally the car drew up outside a large bungalow, with a front garden full of yellow and pink roses, and a tabby cat sprawled out on the windowsill.

"Here we are," Miss Halley said.

I felt Erri stiffen beside me and saw that his hand was clutching the door handle beside him, holding the door shut.

"Give them a chance," I whispered. "Remember, it's only for tea. Perhaps they've got chocolate cake."

The Chesters must have been watching out for the car, because they came out of the door then. I'd expected to hate them, but I didn't. They looked nice and were so pleased to see Erri. Mrs. Chester had black hair, like Erri's, and her eyes were very like his, too, except that hers were hopeful. Her husband was a short man, with a cheerful round face. He was carrying a small kitten in his hands, an absurd-looking creature with a clown's face, patched with black and white and ginger.

I saw Erri look at it. Mr. Chester held it out, asking him if he'd like to hold it, but Erri shook his head. He shook his head at the chocolate cake, too, and sat at the table without once opening his mouth, either to speak or to put food into it.

"Now, come on, Erri," the social worker began, but Mrs. Chester said quickly that it didn't matter.

"If you're not hungry, Erri, perhaps you'd like to leave the table," she suggested. "There're some toys in that box over there."

Erri got down from the table, but he did not go anywhere near the box. He walked straight out of the room and out of the house. I ran after him. He had stopped and was looking at the garden gate. Someone had tacked some chicken wire over the bottom, and the kitten, in trying to climb up it, had gotten one of its claws stuck.

Erri bent down, loosened the kitten's claws from the wire, and picked it up.

"You stupid," he said, sounding very like Victoria.

"Yes, it was," I agreed, "and so were you for refusing the chocolate cake. It was delicious. If you didn't want it, you could've passed it to me under the table."

The social worker was standing in the open doorway, watching us. When she saw me turn to look at her, she stepped back into the shadows.

"I hate them. I not stay," Erri said. Hate was his new word.

"You don't have to stay here if you don't want to. You heard what Miss Halley said. So you might as well enjoy yourself. You can still say no, even if you eat three slices of their chocolate cake."

"Bad cake," Erri said. "Bad people. I hate."

Mrs. Chester had come out of the bungalow and was walking toward us. I hoped she had not heard what he said.

"Oh good, you've got the kitten," she said, smiling. "He's not supposed to go out into the street yet. He hasn't had his inoculations. But you know what young things are like. Always wanting to get out."

Erri didn't say anything, only scowled and handed the kitten to me as if he didn't care for it anymore.

"What's it called?" I asked Mrs. Chester.

"We can't decide on a name," she said. "We want something really nice, something special, but nobody can think of anything. What about you, Erri? Can you think of a name? What shall we call it?"

"Lesley."

It was the first word he'd said to her, and he

spoke rudely, staring at her as if he expected her to object. She didn't, of course. She looked genuinely pleased and said it was a splendid idea. They could call it Les for short. I remembered that the social worker had told my aunt that the Chesters were used to fostering difficult children.

"Let's go in and tell them," she said, and took Erri's hand. I was afraid he'd pull away from her, but he contented himself with looking back at me and making gargoyle faces.

By the end of the visit, he had eaten two slices of chocolate cake and played with the kitten, Les, and we'd all gone out to watch the local kids skateboarding and then to visit the big house in the park and the lake with the black swans. He was quiet and sleepy in the car going home, holding the model airplane they had given him. I thought he was half won over already. He had let Mrs. Chester hug him and kiss the top of his head before he left, doing no more than roll his eyes at me. I didn't know whether to be glad or sorry.

24

It was close to Christmas. The Harwood children would be back, and, best of all, Mum was coming home for good the following week. She was being transferred to her firm's London office, and Auntie Amy had said we could live with her and have the second floor as our own flat.

Isn't she an angel? To have a proper home and a garden again — I can't tell you how I'm looking forward to it, my mother wrote. *I missed you so much, my darling. I'd bring you a camel for Christmas if I could, but they are rather difficult to pack. However, I have bought you a little thing or two.*

Then, like an early Christmas present, Erri was coming to tea. I was glad. Of course I was glad. He is my little brother. And yet . . .

Erri had gone to live with the Chesters at the beginning of October. Although he had agreed to it, at the last moment he changed his mind and cried and clung to me. I had to promise I would come to see him often. I had to promise I would be his foster sister forever.

The social worker frowned a little at this, and when at last Erri had been driven away to his new home, she said to me, "Now we must give him time to settle down with his new foster parents. We mustn't risk upsetting him with visits from old friends too soon."

"If by 'old friend' you mean me, I wouldn't upset him," I told her indignantly. "I promised him I'd visit! I promised! What will he think if I just don't turn up? He'll think I've forgotten him."

She said she had explained it to him. She said she was sure he had understood. She said she knew I would want to do what was best for Erri, wouldn't I?

"Yes, but I know him better than you do. He *needs* me. Everyone needs a friend, and now that Vicky and Robert are away at their schools, there's nobody left but me. I'm his friend, not you." My voice rose. "I am going to visit him. Tomorrow. You can't stop me. I'll take the train. I've got enough money for a ticket."

"Lesley!" Auntie Amy exclaimed. "Be reasonable. Miss Halley didn't mean to upset you. But it's only fair to the Chesters to give them a little time to be by themselves with Erri. Yes, I know he's stayed with them for a couple of nights, but it's not quite the same. He needs a permanent home, and we can't give him that. In a week or two, perhaps —"

"A month or two," the social worker said firmly. "That's what we recommend."

In the end we compromised on three weeks.

Erri had changed when at last I saw him, but perhaps that was a good thing. He was no longer the frightened little ghost of a boy I had seen staring at me from the Harwoods' attic window. He was still thin, but at least now his clothes fit him. His hair was glossy and well cut. He ran laughing down the street outside the Chesters' house with his new friends, and there was color in his cheeks. He did not look so very foreign anymore.

He is safe now, I thought.

Nobody had found out where he came from. Mr. Harwood told us that to all questions about his past, Erri always answered, "I can't remember. I had bad accident. I can't remember this."

"The psychiatrist says he is a fascinating case," Kate said, her blue eyes shining with approval, as if it had been clever of us to have picked out such an interesting child. "Not the amnesia itself, which is fairly straightforward, but the fact that Erri seems to have forgotten his own language, and invariably uses exactly the same words to reject questions. Almost as if somebody had trained him."

I was careful to look only mildly interested, glad that Victoria was not there to catch my eye and make me laugh. Neither of us had owned up. It seemed better to let the psychiatrist remain fascinated. Sometimes I thought Mr. Harwood suspected what we'd done, but he never said anything. Just smiled. I could see why Victoria said most people liked him.

After that first visit, I didn't see Erri very often. He had a bad cold and Mrs. Chester kept him in bed. Then I had a bad cold and my aunt did not want me to go out. But we were both better now, and Mrs. Chester was bringing Erri to have tea with us. I wondered gloomily whether he had wanted to come. He had settled down so well in his new home. I knew I ought to be glad about this. I was glad for him, I really was. But I couldn't help being a little sad for myself. I didn't think he loved me as much as he had. He didn't need me anymore. Still, I had other friends too.

I hurried home from school that day and found that the Harwoods were back. Their terms are shorter than mine. When I saw them last, they had told me we would always be friends. Victoria had said I could be her honorary sister, and Robert had kissed me, claiming it was only a brotherly kiss when Victoria protested. She said I was too young for him to practice on.

"I don't need practice, do I, Lesley?" he'd said and had laughed at me when I blushed.

I told myself now that it would be different when they got back. They might not have forgotten me entirely, but I'd have slipped back to being only the kid next door, someone to smile at when we met and to sell raffle tickets to, not a true friend. But Victoria and Robert were waiting outside, and they ran to greet me, kissing me on both cheeks and hugging me. They told me we were all going to have tea at my house, their mother was already there, and Erri was expected any minute, so we'd better hurry in.

"Both Mum and your aunt have made chocolate cakes for him. Poor Mum's has collapsed," Victoria told me. "But we'd better eat it. She's trying so hard. I wonder what Erri's like now. You've seen him, Lesley. Has he changed?"

"Yes."

"In what way?" she asked.

I hesitated, then said, "He's happier."

Victoria looked at me. Then she said, "What cheek! How dare he be happier without us, the little squirt."

"After all we've done for him," Robert agreed.

"All the cake we've given him," she said.

"All the chocolate —"

"And the paper boat and the kite —"

"And Lesley saved his life! He's got no right to be happy. He ought to be miserable every minute when we're not with him."

I joined in their laughter, liking them very much. "I know," I said lightly, "he's an ungrateful little beast, isn't he? And I bet he eats up all the chocolate cake."

Erri came in, holding Mrs. Chester's hand and pulling back a little. He seemed younger today, a little shy and shuffling. We all said "Hullo! Hullo, Erri!" and he mumbled something back, looking round the room as if he'd never seen it before. Then he looked at me and suddenly smiled. Dropping Mrs. Chester's hand, he ran over to me, holding out a large brown envelope.

"Present," he said, "I bring present for you, Lesley."

It was a handmade Christmas card, a picture of a tricolored kitten with huge green eyes. At the bottom he had printed in wobbly capitals, LUV ERRI. He had learned the word for love, even if he couldn't spell it properly.

"Oh, Erri! It's wonderful!"

I knelt down and hugged him, and he hugged me back. Over his head I could see Victoria and Robert smiling at me.

"Don't be too flattered, Lesley," Victoria said. "It's probably only cupboard love. You're right in front of the chocolate cake."